SIMON

A Story of
Disruption Times

SIMON
A Story of
Disruption Times

George F. MacLean

KNOX PRESS [EDINBURGH]

THE KNOX PRESS (EDINBURGH)
15 North Bank Street, Edinburgh EH1 2LS

❖

© George F. MacLean
First Published 1992

❖

ISBN 0 904422 36 4

❖

Printed by McCorquodale (Scotland) Ltd.

P 59 fright

FOREWORD

18th May 1993 is the 150th Anniversary of the Disruption which brought the Free Church of Scotland into existence in defence of the right of the Church to conduct its own spiritual affairs without interference from law courts or government. This event had widespread consequences for the Church and nation of Scotland.

The Disruption Anniversary Committee appointed by the Free Church General Assembly to arrange for the commemoration of the Disruption commissioned George F. MacLean to produce a book which would introduce younger teenagers to the situation prevailing in 1843. Mr MacLean responded with *Simon*, a work of historical fiction, which looks at the events of these stirring times through the eyes of a Free Church elder's son who became friendly with the daughter of a Church of Scotland minister. It helps to illustrate the way in which the great events of these days affected ordinary human beings and their personal lives and relationships.

Young people who wish a fuller historical account of the Disruption and of the story of the Church in Scotland might be interested in *The Heritage of Our Fathers* by G. N. M. Collins, published by Knox Press.

CONTENTS

Chapter 1

THE REINS OF TERROR

Eeeeeeeeeeeeee! A terrified scream pierced the air. Simon whirled round. At a glance, he took in the scene: a rearing pony and a frantic, white-faced girl in a trap. Then, wild-eyed and with flaring nostrils, the pony bolted. The girl was helpless. She had neither the presence of mind nor the muscle power to control the careering gallop. Jolted from side to side, it took her all her time to stay seated in the trap. She yelled desperately for help above the thunder of the hooves and the rattle and creaking of the trap and, eyes tightly closed, held on for grim death.

As the pony charged towards him and the trap swayed and bounced perilously, Simon stood aghast, rooted to the spot. Then, when the pony was close enough for him to see the bulge of its eyes, he dropped his pannier on the verge of the road and crouched. As the pony galloped past, he sprang and lunged for the reins. One hand scrabbled desperately against the pony's neck but the other hand found its target and tightly grasped the rein. The sudden dive and the wrench on one side of the reins made the pony swerve violently. The girl gave an almighty scream as the trap bucked and tilted. Simon pivoted on the rein and was flung round like a rag doll. At the last moment, the pony swerved again. The trap momentarily mounted the verge and the wheel hub of the trap scraped the wooden fence which ran along the road.

With the pony back on a straight course but heading for a tight corner in the road, Simon was dragged backwards along the road. Sparks flew from the iron heel-plates of his boots. The socket of his arm ached agonisingly as the free arm flailed, trying to get a hold on the rein.

His fingers closed on leather. Simon managed to pull himself round to see where the pony was heading. There was no time to lose if the pony was to be slowed down before the corner. Otherwise the trap was bound to topple over on the corner and throw the girl out. If only he could reach the bridle. He would never be able to reach the other rein. He heaved on the rein with all his might. The pony's head swung to the left and Simon grabbed for the bridle. He missed. Again he heaved and missed. It was no use. He pulled his knees up and hung on the rein. Yes, the pony was slowing but still galloping.

Perilously fast, the pony and trap swung into the corner. The trap swayed, tilted and teetered on one wheel. The wheel bumped on the verge, knocking the trap back onto two wheels with a bone-jarring clatter. Tossed from one side to the other, the girl clung to her seat in the trap.

Gradually, as it straightened out of the corner and went into a straight stretch of road, the pony slowed to a canter and then to a trot. Eventually, Simon managed to get the pony halted. Its sides heaved and its nostrils quivered as Simon eased his hand off the rein and massaged his aching shoulder before jumping up to see the girl in the trap.

Shaking with fear, she managed a wan smile.

"That wis a close ane, Miss. Are ye alricht? Ye're shaking all over."

"I've had quite a fright but I'll be fine when I get my breath back. No doubt I'll be aching all over tomorrow, but what does that matter? I'm alive and have nothing serious wrong with me. I owe my life to you." Her brown eyes under the smudged silk bonnet shone with gratitude.

"Och, it was nothin'," Simon mumbled, embarrassed by this pretty, well-spoken lass and her emotion.

"I suppose you do this every day," she laughed, further increasing his confusion. "I'm sorry. I shouldn't tease you after you risked your life for me. You're an extremely brave fellow and very strong."

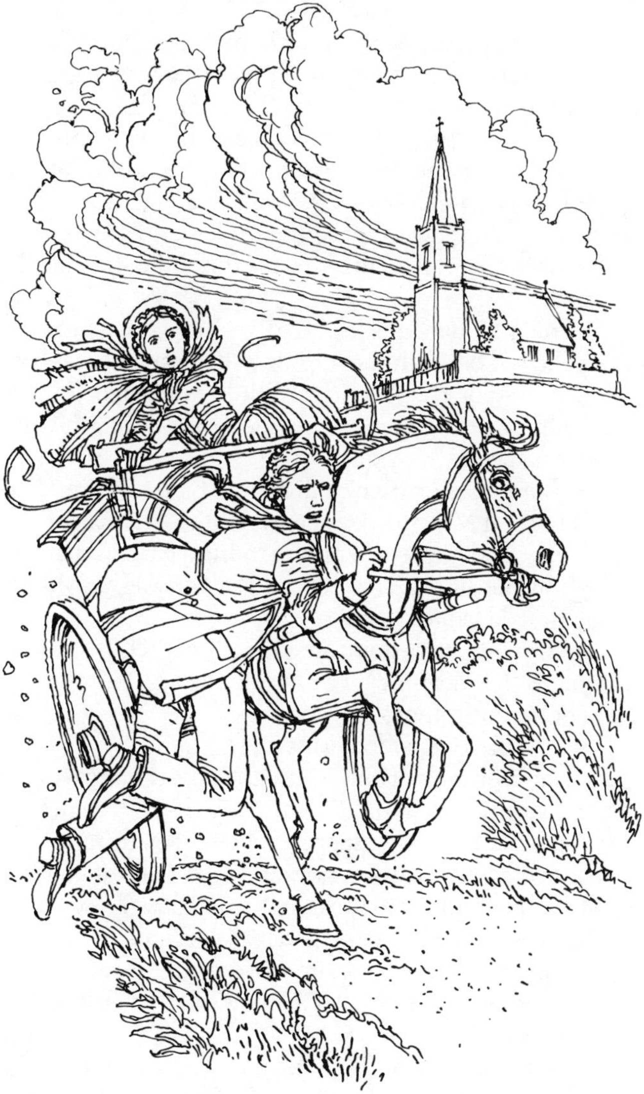

Simon had recovered some of his composure. "Were ah tae dae this every day ah suppose ah'd soon grow strong. But I dinna make a habit o' rescuin' pretty lassies. How did the pony bolt!"

"I was going to visit two old ladies and give them some shawls I made. All of a sudden a swarm of bees started buzzing about the pony's head and it must have panicked."

"Here, ah shouldnae be keepin' bletherin' tae ye when ye've had such an awful fright. Ah'll tak the bridle and walk the pony home for ye."

The girl stiffened. "No, I'll be fine. If my father finds out I'll not be allowed out with the trap again. He's an old dear but he is a bit of a fusspot. I hope you don't think me dreadful for saying that. I really have forgotten my manners today. I haven't asked you your name yet."

"Simon. Simon Shaw. Ah'm from Braeside Farm. Ah'm still a scholar at Millerton Academy. Whit's your name?"

"Annabel Ferguson. I'm from the next parish, Auchengarve."

"Auchengarve? An ye've come all the way tae Millerton tae gie twa old ladies shawls?"

Annabel stiffened and drew herself up. "If I choose to do that, what is to hinder me?" Her face flushed and it was not due to her recent alarming escapade.

"Ah beg your pardon, Miss."

Annabel stared at him and then softened. She gave a mischievous laugh. "Oh, don't take me too seriously. I sometimes flare up, just like my pony, I suppose, but most of the time I am good-natured." She became serious. "I was actually taking a detour. My father thinks I am too religious and doesn't like my visits to the poor souls who are so grateful to see me."

"Ah see, Miss. Ah admire ye for that."

"Well, well. We are full of admiration for each other," laughed Annabel. "I must go."

Simon leapt down from the trap. Annabel flicked the reins rather nervously and the pony, now calm, moved off at a leisurely pace.

Simon turned back to where he had thrown his pannier. His own legs felt quite wobbly underneath him. Annabel would be pretty shaky too when she got home. Funny how he thought of her as Annabel and not Miss Ferguson. Quite a spirited lass in her own way.

Simon groaned when he saw his pannier, even although he had been expecting something like it. The eggshells, of course, had cracked. The egg-white and yolk had transmogrified the pure white crowdie wrapped in muslin into soggy, gooey yellow lumps. Even the carrots were covered in the yellow slime. Who would buy that at a market? Perhaps the carrots could be washed in the Mill Burn. All this would require some explaining when he got home. He could just hear his mother's voice: "Gie him some books or gie him some problem tae work out and there's nae anither lad tae touch him, but gie him somethin' ordinary or practical tae dae an' he's sure tae botch it…"

DIFFICULT WORDS

Page 1	– pannier	*a basket carried on the back*
Page 4	– detour	*roundabout way*
Page 5	– transmogrified	*horribly changed*
	– muslin	*a fine cotton cloth*

Chapter 2

ANNABEL'S IDENTITY

Simon was right. His visit to the market had been decidedly unsuccessful. The well-washed carrots had sold for satisfactory prices despite the amused comments.

"Aye," observed one red-faced farm worker with huge leathery hands, "they scholars canna bide a wee bit dirt. Even their carrots hae tae wash themsels at the pump evra morn."

The rest of the produce had to be covered from view before he was exposed to real ridicule. If he told them what really had happened, not only would he be acutely embarrassed but he would most certainly have been branded a romancer and liar of the most extravagant and fanciful variety.

His mother's reaction had been equally predictable. She scolded him mercilessly, demanding an explanation and launching a salvo of accusations and denunciations before he had time to draw breath, far less give an account of himself.

"... sic a daft gowk in a' ma days. It must be a' the schoolin' yir gettin' that's makin' you sae saft in the heid. An' how can we afford tae keep ye in school wi'oot money? An' how are we tae get money when ye canna sell a few things at the market, pray tell?"

Simon was rescued by his father's appearance.

"Whit's a' this aboot, then?" demanded Simon's father. He was fresh in from the fields. He had taken off his boots but had yet to wash. Sweat stained his flannel shirt. His working trousers were flecked with wisps of hay and stray animal hairs. He was of medium height but sturdy build. He was a fair but no-nonsense man. The piercing stare of his grey eyes could make the guilty tremble.

6

"He's just a daft gowk, that's all," snapped Simon's mother. "Ye canna send him on the simplest o' errands but he makes a total muck o't. He comes back here frae the market wi' a few pence for the carrots and a soggy mish-mash o' egg and crowdie. A' ma hard work for nothin' yet we still have tae keep the useless lump at his books. It's a disgrace, ah tell ye! If ah ..."

"Ah hae a guid explanation, Faither, but Mither widnae listen tae me. Ah didnae hae a chance tae explain."

"Alricht, get on wi' it then."

So Simon started explaining what had happened. Both his parents were silent. The indignant look on his mother's face gradually softened as the story progressed. His father's face stayed expressionless until he mentioned the name Miss Annabel Ferguson.

"Whit did ye say her name was?" his father asked.

"Annabel Ferguson. Why?"

"Ah think ah'm richt when ah say that her faither is the parish minister in Auchengarve."

"But she said that her faither told her that she was tae religious," objected Simon. "How could she be a minister's dochter?"

"Ye've a lot tae learn, lad. Auld Ferguson is a Moderate. But by the sound o't his dochter's nae a Moderate."

"A Moderate? Whit's that?"

"Ah did tell ye that ye had a lot tae learn. A' ministers are nae like Mr Gillespie. Whit's a Moderate? Jist the verra opposite o' Mr Gillespie. Mr Gillespie is a holy man o' God. The Moderates are worldly men. Mr Gillespie loves souls. Most Moderates care more for their stipend or glebe than they do for souls. Mr Gillespie preaches wi' warmth and power. Most Moderates read out some sermon full o' fine language that naebody wi' a bit dung on their boots wid understand. Mr Gillespie is full o' zeal for the gospel. The Moderates cannae stick that sort o' thing. They dae a' they can tae stop any new churches bein' built in the new toons that are sproutin' like weeds on a vegetable patch."

"Ah rescued a minister's dochter? She was a bonny lass – a richt lady."

"In that case ye can forget a' aboot her. Studies or no studies, she'd niver look at the likes o' ye," put in Simon's mother. "Alricht, it wisnae ye tae blame for whit happened tae the eggs and crowdie. It couldnae be helped. Ah should hae listened tae ye afore scoldin' ye like yon. Ye were verra brave. But dinna ye start wi' daft romantic notions about Miss Annabel Ferguson."

"Ah'm no exactly Romeo, mither."

"As long as ye keep that in mind, Simon. By the way, whit happened when ye got tae the market?"

Simon's father laughed heartily at Simon's account of the derisive comments on the washed carrots and his squirming anxiety over the possible discovery of the soggy yellow crowdie. Simon was beginning to enjoy narrating his adventures now that he knew his mother's wrath had fizzled out.

❊   ❊   ❊   ❊

That night Simon dreamed confused, fantastic dreams. He was being trampled under hooves. Then he was being nursed by Annabel. He had cold, yellow, slimy stuff placed on bandages over his bruises. A portly gentleman with a white cravat and gold watch and chain roared with anger when Annabel put a bandage on him. Annabel grabbed some shawls and ran off. The man's face loomed over him. Bees started to swarm over it and the man yelled and ran away. A man with big red hands and fingers like stumpy carrots tried to sell him crowdie and eggs. Then his mother appeared yelling at the man, "What are you doing with my crowdie and eggs?" Then Simon woke up in a sweat. He wiped the beads of sweat off his upper lip, groaned, turned over and drifted off into more but still restless sleep.

In the morning he was stiff and sore. His head was fuzzy and he could only remember vaguely the chaos of his disordered dreams.

DIFFICULT WORDS

Page 6	– salvo	*a burst of fire from guns*
Page 7	– stipend	*minister's salary*
	– glebe	*land attached to a manse*
Page 8	– Romeo	*character in a play by Shakespeare who falls in love*

Chapter 3

CRISIS IN THE KIRK

The heavy oak door flew open. A blast of wind scattered the feathers Simon's Mum had plucked from the hen she held in her lap. As her husband stood shaking the snow off his coat, she called, "Dinnae mind the snaw, Andrew. Jist come awe in and shut that door. That wind is like tae freeze the verra marrow o' ma bones. Whit happened at the manse?"

"There's a meetin in the nicht after next. It's goin tae be addressed by a deputation. They are goin tae explain aboot a' the trouble in the kirk an' yon big meetin they had in Edinburgh – a convocation or somethin' like that."

"Ah dinna follow a' they big words. Why can't they preach their sermons in Kirk and let things be?"

"Why can the government nae let things be?" retorted Simon's Dad. "Why can the law nae let the kirk see tae its own affairs? It's because the Kirk is bossed aboot by Landlords and Lairds that there's a' this commotion. Tak Rev. Ferguson, for example."

"Whit aboot him? He's a clever man, is he nae?"

"Aye, he's clever. But the people didnae want him and little could they dae aboot it. Sir Andrew Strachan had put his name forward an' that was a' aboot it as far as the law was concerned. The people couldnae dae a thing aboot it. They werenae allowed tae choose their ain minister. But auld Ferguson fairly had it hot the nicht o' the induction."

Simon walked into the room for a break from his studies. "Ferguson? Whit are ye talkin' aboot?" he said.

"Ah was talkin' aboot the time when the Reverend Ferguson

was made the minister of Auchengarve."

"Whit aboot it?"

"Well, the people a' thocht him a richt Moderate an' were determined no' tae hae him as their minister. Oor ain minister was agin him but the rest o' the ministers in the Presbytery were happy enought tae see him inducted. On the nicht o' the induction the Presbytery arrived wi' Mister Ferguson an' a body o' constables. A' the people were gathered round the kirk but naebody could get in. Someone had taken the keys o' the kirk and had hidden them. There was a lot o' jeering' an' laughin at the Presbytery. They were in a richt fix. They stood there wi' faces like frightened ghosts and whispered amang themsels."

"Whit did they dae?" asked Simon. "Did they run like rabbits?"

"Ah'll gie them credit for that," said Simon's Dad. "Shaken they micht hae been, but they stood their ground. Auld Reverend Bruce frae Carnock – he's well named, ah tell ye, and he fought under the Duke o' Wellington against Napoleon – well, he barked oot tae the constables, 'Smash a window, I say. You are officers of the law and this is a legally appointed Presbytery meeting. No riotous mob will keep me from my duty.' Well, you can imagine the uproar that caused. But then Mr Gillespie stepped forward. Jist like a class o' noisy scholars wid be quelled by an angry glance frae the schoolmaister, the hubbub died down. The Reverend Gillespie was a great favourite."

"Aye, an' he still is," commented Simon's Mum. "But as sure as ma name's Bessie Shaw ah cannae picture him standin' up tae a yellin' mob."

"Frail-lookin' he may be –"

"Frail?" interrupted Simon's Mum. "There's mair meat on a hen's claws. Ah wonder the slightest wind disnae blow him aff like thistle-down."

"He hasnae got a strong voice, either. Thin though it was, it didnae waver an' ah tell ye that by the time he was finished there was a lot o' shufflin' o' feet and lowered eyes. Ah've never seen sae mony red faces and sheepish looks in ma life."

"Why, whit did he say, Faither?" asked Simon.

"Ah cannae recall a' that he said but he started off commenting on the number there. There were far mair than were usually there on the Sabbath day. Whit was taking them there? he asked. They had never shown concern for their own souls, far less for the Kirk."

"That was a guid ane," said Simon's Mum appreciatively.

"Aye, but he was jist gettin' warmed up. 'No man believes more strongly than I do in the right of a congregation to call its own minister,' he said. 'But no one believes more strongly that your unruly behaviour brings disgrace upon yourselves and does damage to those who wish to promote your rights.' He's aye had a grand way wi' words had Mr Gillespie. Then he put the case against them as powerfully as any advocate frae Edinburgh. They wid hae the kirk desecrated before they would surrender the key, they showed contempt for the authority o' the Kirk and o' the law, they broke the scriptures which told us tae live peaceably with all men an' tae adorn the doctrine of our Lord Jesus Christ with holy lives an' finally they were little better than common thieves because they had stolen the key o' the kirk. He had jist finished speakin' when a voice shouted oot that the key was under a certain stane. A constable was sent tae fetch the key an' open the kirk."

"Aye, they micht well hae been sheepish," remarked Simon's Mum. "In fact ah think they were jist a lot o' goats."

"Sheepish or nae, there wisnae mair than ten men oot o' a' the parish who entered the kirk that nicht or for mony a long day afterwards. An' ah can tell ye, Bessie, that had ah been in the parish o' Auchengarve ah wid hae been ane o' them that widnae hae listened tae the cauld morality o' a graceless moderate."

"Ye were aye heidstrong, Robert Shaw."

"That may well be, my lass, but ah hae my principles an' as far as ah see it's nae a bad thing tae be thrawn where yir principles are concerned."

"Well, ane o' my principles is tae hae my work a' done an' tae be in my bed in guid time tae rise early. Ye menfolk are aye goin' on aboot the womenfolk bletherin' but it'd tak a lot tae beat ye when ye get goin'. Ye'd talk the nicht away."

"Ah winnae keep ye back, lassie." Simon's father paused thoughtfully. "Simon, there's goin' tae be an important meetin' the nicht after next. It's aboot a' the troubles in the Kirk. There are rumours of a split in the Kirk. Dae ye want tae come wi' me?"

Simon's eyes shone. He needed no second invitation. Sitting at his books night after night could be a very dreary business. But what really pleased him was that his father was treating him as a man, as someone who was responsible and was concerned for the great affairs of the nation's Kirk.

DIFFICULT WORDS

Page 10	– deputation	*a group appointed to state a point of view*
	– induction	*service at which a minister is appointed to a congregation*

Page 11 – Presbytery   *the minister and selected elders from an area*
Page 12 – advocate   *lawyer qualified to present a case in a court of law*

        – desecrated   *shown disrespect for something holy*
        – morality   *teachings about what is right and wrong*

Chapter 4

CONTROVERSY

The huge barn was packed with people. Young men were perched on rafters and had scrambled up on to a threshing mill. Others, not to be outdone and wishing a similar vantage point, were positioned up the ladders used to obtain access to the barn loft. The elderly sat on bales of straw but most of the people were standing. The warm, musty smell of straw and hay filled the barn. Oil lamps burned at intervals on the walls.

The excitement in the barn was as great as that at the announcement of the results at an election for Parliament. The laird had gone to the sheriff in order to prevent the church being used by the deputation of speakers who were to explain their opposition to the interference of the law and of the government in what they considered the affairs of the church. The sheriff had prohibited the meeting by issuing an interdict forbidding the use of the church by the deputation. However, despite the law and despite the laird's threats, a farmer was found who granted the use of his barn and the attempt to stop the meeting only caused greater interest in it. In the bothies and in the fields, in the maids' quarters and in the milking sheds, in the mill and in the smiddy, all the talk had been of the deputation.

Simon and his Dad had gone early to secure a good stance and were positioned by the barn wall near the front. A sudden hush fell over the people, followed by a buzz of excited whispering and turning of heads.

"Whit's happened, Faither?" hissed Simon.

"Did ye nae see who is standin' at the back o' the barn? That's him tae the richt o' the door. It's the Reverend Ferguson frae Auchengarve."

15

"Is that him wi' the red face and the lace cravat?"

"Well, it's nae a ploughman, that's for sure," snorted Simon's Dad.

"Whit's he daein' here, Faither?"

"Well, ah dinnae richtly ken but ah'm sure it's nae tae gie his blessing tae the deputation. It may jist be curiosity, but ah widnae be surprised if he wid try tae coup the cairt we're travellin' in."

There was another hush. The deputation had arrived. Led by the Reverend Gillespie, the deputation made its way through the thronging people to the front. Mr Gillespie stood on a cart which served as a platform. He announced a psalm and one of the deputation party led the singing in a melodious but slightly wavering voice. The singing rose and fell in great rhythmical surges. The earnestness and determination in his father's voice as he sang the words:

> God in the midst of her doth dwell;
> Nothing shall her remove

really gripped Simon. When the last note of their singing had died down, the Reverend Gillespie prayed. His theme was the faithfulness of God and the faithfulness of those of the past who had suffered for the testimony of Jesus. He then welcomed the Reverend Dr Paterson and the Reverend Buchan who were to speak. He also called attention to the presence of the Reverend Ferguson and welcomed him.

"Mr Gillespie!" boomed a voice from the back. All heads turned. "If I may, I would like to address a few words to you."

Mr Gillespie did not hesitate. "I would have preferred, Mr Ferguson, that you had waited till the deputation had been able to address the meeting before speaking, but, if you keep your remarks brief, you may say a few words."

"Thank you, Mr Gillespie. I have decided to come along because there have come into our midst those who are the troublers of Israel. In the last few years there has been the undignified spectacle of the church being dragged through the law courts and defying the highest legal body of our land, the Court of Session. What example is that to give to the people of our land?

Now the scriptures tell us plainly that we are to live in subjection to those who are in authority. The spirit of those who have called this meeting is not one of submissiveness but of rebellion because they have defied an interdict granted by the sheriff forbidding the meeting.

We have the great privilege of having men like our own laird who contribute greatly from their own pockets to the upkeep of church buildings and the stipends of ministers. Were it not for such, the kirks of our land would be in a sorry condition and their ministers as poor as the proverbial church mice.

The recent Convocation which met in Edinburgh is set upon the ruin of our national church. It is determined to split the Kirk of which we are all proud. It was a gathering of hot-heads and malcontents. I appeal to you all to leave this gathering now before you minds are poisoned with their smooth talk and the

Kirk is brought to ruin."

It was a critical moment. Would anyone get up and start a mass exodus from the meeting? Mr Ferguson's voice was powerful and melodious. His appeal to scripture was a clever move and he had exploited the affection which the people had for the Kirk of their fathers.

Simon felt his father stiffen. His hands were tightly clenched and his lips were quivering. Was his father about to intervene and answer the Reverend Ferguson?

Simon's suspense was cut short by the voice of Mr Gillespie. Always thin it appeared even more so after the deep, strong voice of Mr Ferguson.

"Mr Ferguson, thank you for your contribution. Before I ask Dr Paterson to speak, I wish to make a few comments.

Had you known your Bible better, Mr Ferguson, you would not have called us troublers of Israel. It was the wicked King Ahab who first used that term of the prophet Elijah. We are no more troubling the Kirk then Elijah was troubling Israel.

Had you known your Bible better, too, you would not have urged us to submit to those in authority when they are intent on destroying the freedom and independence of the Kirk. Did Peter not say that we ought to obey God rather than men when the authorities of his day tried to deny gospel freedoms?

We are not guilty of breaking the interdict, Mr Ferguson. That prohibited us, not from meeting, but for meeting in the kirk.

I commend to Mr Ferguson another study: that of the history of the Kirk. He will learn from the famous Andrew Melville's remarks to the foxy and Kirk-hating King James VI that there are two kingdoms in Scotland. One kingdom is a spiritual kingdom. Neither Laird nor Monarch, neither Parliament nor Court of Session has the right to overrule the Church in spiritual matters. And if determination to uphold that right is thought a malicious intention to split the Kirk, then those who think so show that they would prefer the Kirk to be the servant of worldly powers than the servant of King Jesus.

If the just desires of the Kirk are disregarded, we may have to separate from the Kirk to maintain our independence. We will do so with broken hearts. And we will do so in the full knowledge that there will be hard times ahead for ministers and their flocks. But we will do so in the knowledge that the God who sustained the Kirk in the dark days of the Killing Times when the faithful were persecuted and harried and mercilessly killed will most certainly keep us in all our difficulties."

There was another silence. Then thunderous cheering broke out. Even though Mr Gillespie had raised his hand for silence, it was several minutes before the cheering had died down. When Simon, who had been carried away and had shouted himself hoarse with the rest of the gathering, looked round, there was no sign of Mr Ferguson. He had taken advantage of the uproar to slip out and beat a hasty retreat.

DIFFICULT WORDS

Page 17	– subjection	*under the rule*
	– submissiveness	*willingness to obey authority*
	– malcontents	*discontented troublemakers*
Page 18	– exodus	*outflow*
	– melodious	*musical*
	– exploited	*made clever use of*
Page 19	– Killing Times	*a period when the Covenanters were persecuted*
	– harried	*constantly attacked*

Chapter 5

LEARNING LEADS THE WAY

The meeting held by the deputation had made a great impression on Simon. It was not simply the drama of the Reverend Ferguson's intervention which had impressed him. He had listened avidly to the account they gave of the measures the evangelicals were taking; printing and selling 150,000 one penny newsletters each week; drawing up plans for a special fund called a Sustentation Fund which would be a special fund from which all the ministers would be paid; and holding prayer times every Saturday night in every evangelical manse in Scotland. The clear explanation of the situation by the deputation, their assurance of the rightness of their cause, their calm acceptance of the hardships which lay ahead – all these had captured not only his imagination but his heart. His own faith and sense of commitment to Christ had been greatly deepend. He had been drawn into the greatest issue of his day in Scotland.

Strangely enough, his interest in the crisis in the Church of Scotland did not harm his studies. Rather, it helped them. The desire had formed in his heart to serve Christ and, if possible, to become a minister. He had told no-one about it, but had thrown himself into his studies with much greater enthusiasm than he had ever shown before.

One day when the frost was keen and one's breath misted the air, Simon was surprised to see the Headmaster approach him. A stern disciplinarian, the sight of his hooked nose, flowing white whiskers and piercing eyes made the most dare-devil of pupils check their bravado.

"Simon Shaw, you will come to my room after morning prayers," barked Mr Maitland.

"Y-yes, sir," stammered Simon. What had he done wrong?

"Don't look so worried, Shaw. You are not in trouble."

"Thank you, sir. Will I report to Mr Finlay first?"

"Just come straight to my room."

"Yes, Sir."

Simon's mind was in a whirl so that he could not concentrate properly at prayers. What did old Maitland want?

Simon stood at the door where so many had stood with dried-up mouths and sweating palms. The headmaster strode briskly to the door and opened it. "Just come in, Shaw."

Simon entered the room and glanced around. Two paintings of grim-faced headmasters of past eras in the life of the school hung on the wall behind the headmaster's leather-inlaid desk. A spare black academic gown hung on a peg. Leather-bound books lined one wall. On the wall opposite, a small window let in the pale winter light. Under it a globe of the world stood on top of an ornately carved cupboard.

The headmaster placed a plain wooden chair in front of his desk and motioned to Simon to take a seat. He himself stood looking out the window with his hands behind his back.

After a moment or two he went to his desk and sat down. "I have noticed recently that there has been a marked improvement in your work, Simon." Simon noted the use of his first name. Usually Mr Maitland called the pupils by their surname. This was a good sign. "Indeed, you show considerable promise."

Simon felt himself blush. "Th-thank you, sir."

"Really, Shaw, I wish you would learn to control that stammer. It irritates me." Simon wished that he could too. He thought it was because he had to switch from the Scots which was natural for him to the English which was used in school and in polite society. If he was unsure of himself or embarrassed or excited he always stammered in English. He rarely ever did that in Scots.

"As I was saying, you show promise. Now to come to the point. I would like you to go to university. How would your parents view that?"

Simon paused a moment, both to think and to make sure that he did not stammer. "I'm not very sure, sir. They would probably like me to but -"

"I will see your father about this. I am sure that I can persuade him. He is a man of good sense.

Now, there is stumbling block. You will need to do well at Greek and though you have made considerable improvement you will need to make further advances.

I have no doubt that you can make that progress. But Mr Finlay is not a well man. He will not be returning to the school and no replacement can be found for him who is able to teach Greek. I will set work for your class and teach it when I am able but you need more than that.

I am on good terms with the Reverend Ferguson of Auchengarve. I have no doubt but that he will agree to tutor you. He is an execllent Greek scholar. In fact," grunted Mr Maitland, "he would find it easier to quote Sophocles than Solomon. Do you wish to have his services?"

Simon was stunned. Try as he did, he could not control the stammer. "W-would I have to go to the manse at Auchengarve?"

"But of course, lad. Did you think that Mr Ferguson would have to travel to your farm as well as teach you Greek?"

"No, sir. I would be very grateful if you would arrange it, sir. Will I have to pay Mr Ferguson?"

"Don't worry yourself about that, Simon. I will see both Mr Ferguson and your father. Now off you go to your class."

"Thank you, sir. I am very grateful to you."

Simon did not know what to think as he trudged home after school. What a fool he had made of himself by asking if he would have to go to the manse at Auchengarve! He blushed at the very thought of his stupidity and aimed a kick at a stone which landed with a satisfying *clonk* on a stone dike.

His mother would be proud to think of him as a student at

unversity but she was always complaining about his having his head in a book when he could be doing something useful? And could his parents really afford it?

Would he be able to cope with university? He was just a country lad with none of the airs and graces of the city dwellers. Would he just be lost and miserable?

What would it be like going to the manse at Auchengarve? Would the Reverend Ferguson remember seeing him at the deputation meeting from which the minister had scurried with his tail between his legs? Would he then take a dislike to Simon? Would Simon see the spirited Annabel at the manse?

What did old Maitland mean by saying that he didn't need to worry about paying Mr Ferguson? Oh, it was all too much for him to sort out!

Going up the rutted farm track, Simon decided that the best policy was to say nothing. After all, Mr Maitland had said that he would speak to his father.

DIFFICULT WORDS

Page 20 – avidly   *eagerly*
         – evangelical   *believing strongly in sin, atonement by*
                             Christ and the need for personal faith
Page 21 – eras   *stages or times*
         – ornately   *in a highly decorated style*
Page 22 – Sophocles   *an ancient Greek dramatist*
         – Solomon   *King of Israel and writer of proverbs*

Chapter 6

AT THE MANSE

The Auchengarve manse dominated the country round about. It was situated on a hill overlooking fairly flat agricultural land. Had those who so situated it thought of it as a sentinel on watch looking out for the evil influences which might harm the people or had they seen it as a vantage point from which a minister might yearn for his people's salvation, much as Jesus had yearned to see the people of Jerusalem accept him as their Messiah?

Simon did not have such exalted thoughts as he walked up the tree-lined driveway to the manse. In the first place, he was overwhelmed by the size and grandeur of the manse. Two great round pillars supported a canopy over the huge front door and round them twined the thorny, leafless steams of a climbing rose. Each window was arched with ornamental stonework at the top of its arch. Two wings gave the building a pleasing symmetry. Little wonder that Mr Maitland had been astounded at the thought of the Reverend Ferguson going to Simon's farmhouse. Why, Simon might have thought that he had come to the Laird's mansion rather than to the manse had he not been given such clear directions.

Secondly, he was frightened of Mr Ferguson. If he was such a clever man, would he not think Simon a plodding dimwit? What if Mr Ferguson recognised him as one of those present at the meeting in the barn?

Simon pulled the bell and heard a faint musical tinkling deep within the manse. After a few seconds footsteps came to the door. Simon held his breath. The door opened. It was a maid. She was plain-looking, but had a rounded, cheery face.

"Maister Shaw, is it? The minister wis expectin' ye. Ye'll find

25

c

him in the study. It's the second door on the left."

She led him up the deeply carpeted hallway and knocked on the study door.

"Come in!" called a deep voice which Simon recalled from the unforgettable night of the meeting in the barn.

The maid opened the door. "It's Maister Shaw tae see ye, Mister Ferguson."

"Thank you, Annie. Come away in, Simon. I'm glad to meet someone with an interest in Greek. I'm very fond of it myself."

"It – it's very good of you to give the time to help me", said Simon.

"Nonsense! I'm glad to be able to help. That's what we are here for, after all. God put us here to help one another. Now let's get down to business. What have you been studying? ..."

An hour later, the door of the study swung open and Annabel swept in.

"Father, I have just received an invitation from – Oh, I did not realise you had someone with you."

"It's all right, Annabel. Simon will probably be glad of a break from the tedium of Greek constructions. Have you met Annabel, Simon?"

Simon was shot a warning glance by Annabel. What could he say? He couldn't tell a lie yet he could get Annabel into trouble if he told the truth.

"I – I'm sure Miss Annabel doesn't move in the same circles as I do. She won't mix with farm girls and servant lassies." Where Simon got the inspiration to avoid a direct answer he didn't know.

"Huh! I'm not so sure about that. She's so soft-hearted and so much of a religious enthusiast she would give her shoes to a beggar and walk home bare-foot." Mr Ferguson was obviously onto a hobby-horse.

Annabel tossed her head and her dark eyes flashed. "That's a fine way to speak of your daughter in front of a stranger. Doesn't the Bible say, "Blessed is he that considereth the poor?" You really are forgetting yourself, father. You have not introduced me yet."

Rather ashamed of himself for provoking this outburst and for his lack of social grace, Mr Ferguson apologised. "You are quite right, Annabel. I was forgetting myself. Simon, this is my daughter Annabel. Annabel, this is Simon Shaw from Millerton Academy. His teacher is ill and as Simon is a promising student I have agreed to tutor him in Greek."

Annabel had softened. "I am very pleased to welcome you to the manse, Simon. Father, it is very good of you to help Simon. I should not have spoken so sharply to you."

"Annabel, you were quite right, as I said."

"Father, I will speak to you later about the invitation I have received. Goodbye, Simon. I hope father doesn't bore you to death with Greek." With a mischievous little laugh she added, "He's such an enthusiast!" She made a swift exit, closing the door softly behind her.

"Annabel, as you can see, is a very headstrong girl and has a quick and able tongue, but I am very fond of her. Now, back to our studies. Where were we? ..."

"Well, Simon, you did well today and I am sure with a little perseverance you will master Greek and find that it becomes a pleasure rather than a chore." He rang a bell. "The maid will show you out."

"Thank you, sir. I am very grateful."

The door opened and the maid entered.

"Show Master Shaw out, please, Miss Reid."

Simon was shown out. As he walked down the manse drive to the ornamental stone pillars which marked the start of the drive, his mind was less on Greek than on Annabel. How that little episode in the study had reminded him of the day when he had rescued her! She had seemed even more beautiful. She had an energy and vitality quite different to the boisterousness of some of the country lassies.

He was startled out of his thoughts as he passed out of the gates.

"Simon!"

There, walking along behind the tall hedge which adjoined the great pillars was Annabel.

"I want to thank you properly for that day you saved my life. I have often thought of that day since."

"That's strange," said Simon. "I was just thinking of that day as I walked down the driveway. You had the same spark in you that day as you had today when your father got on to you."

"Well, that's a nice thing for you to say, Simon Shaw," she laughed.

"Aye, but it's true. Anyway, it makes you more attractive." Simon blushed as he said it.

She regarded him steadily with her brown eyes. "I believe you mean that Simon. Anyway, it's father's attention I shall attract if I detain you any longer. Goodbye, Simon."

"Goodbye, Annabel."

As Annabel strolled away and Simon turned to make his way home, he was even more deeply in thought than he had been when he was walking down the drive.

DIFFICULT WORDS

Page 25 – sentinel   *guard*
        – canopy   *a roof projecting out to form a shelter*
Page 27 – constructions   *the ways words are put together in a language*

Chapter 7

CATACLYSM IN THE KIRK

Simon fidgeted constantly until he got on his mother's nerves. She threatened to tie him to a chair. She poked fun at him.

"Perhaps ye've got ants in yir breeks. Dinnae say that ye've got fleas!" she said in mock horror. "Perhaps ye're worryin' aboot that Annabel ye're always talkin' aboot," she added slyly.

"Mither, ye ken fine why ah cannae rest. How can ye be sae calm when the hale o' Scotland is agog tae see whit has happened in the Kirk?"

"Well, whit will be will be. It's up tae a' those ministers and elders gathered at the General Assembly tae decide, nae tae the likes o' me. If ah were tae worry aboot it, there'd be nae socks washed or butter churned."

"Well, ah cannae help it, mither. Ah wish ah could hae gone tae Edinburgh wi' my Faither."

"Yir studies come first. If ye were tae galavant tae Edinburgh jist noo, ye micht nae be goin' there tae university. Mind ye, it wis yir Faither that wanted ye tae gang tae university. Ah wid hae been quite happy tae see ye get a job and earn an honest penny."

"Ah dinnae think Faither will be hame the nicht. Perhaps he will be tomorrow. Ah cannae wait."

"Well, ye'll jist hae tae," responsed Simon's Mum drily. "In the meantime, fetch twa logs an' pit them on the fire."

❋   ❋   ❋   ❋

Simon bounded up when he heard the clatter of hooves and the creak and rattle of the trap. He dashed out, hurdling over the grey cat which was stretching itself on the cobbles and scattering squawking hens left and right.

"Quick Faither, whit happened?"

"Steady on, lad. It's a wonder ye didnae startle the horse and coup the trap. Ye cam oot o' that farmhoose like there wis a legion o' witches at yir tail. Well, lad, tae answer yir question, the Kirk has split. A great division has taken place. But ah've got tae unharness the horse an' see him attended tae first. Ah've been on the road for mony a weary mile. Ask yir mither tae prepare somethin' tasty."

"Richt, Faither," replied Simon and turned to go to the farmhouse. So it had happened. Even though he had fully expected it, the news still came as a shock. What would happen to the Reverend Gillespie? What would his father do? How would the new Kirk obtain the money to pay its ministers? Where would those who joined it worship? His head was whirling as he went into the kitchen.

"Mither, Faither is here. The Kirk has split!"

His mother was silent for a few moments. Then she sighed. "Well, it had tae be. Ah'll jist get the broth heated up for yir faither and pit a few tatties on."

Simon's Dad licked his lips appreciatively. "There's nae a woman in a' the land can mak a better plate o' broth than ye, Bessie. Ah feel the better for it."

"Oh, ah can mak a guid pan o' broth all richt," said Simon's Mum, "but so can only farmer's wife who's worth her salt," she added modestly.

"Faither, ah'm burstin' tae hear mair aboot whit happened at the Assembly. Are ye ready tae tell us?"

Before Simon's Dad could say a word there came a knock at the kitchen door. Simon's Mum went to see who was there. There stood a tall, brown-faced, gap-toothed man with a slight squint in his left eye.

"Oh, it's yirsel, Archie. Come awe in. Dae ye want a bite tae eat?"

"Nae thanks, Missus Shaw. Ah wis jist wonderin' how yir man

got on in Edinburgh. My missus said tae me, 'Archie, ye're a richt ane. Did ye nae ken that curiosity killed the cat?' So ah said tae her, 'Aye, an' did ye no hear o' the sayin' aboot the pot callin' the kettle black? Besides, satisfaction revived the cat.' So ah winnae stay but for a few minutes."

"Jist tak a seat. Ah'll give ye a cup o' tea."

"Come in, Archie. It's guid tae see ye. Ah'm sure it's nae aboot sowin' neeps or hoein' tatties that ye've come tae see me." Simon's Dad knew that he would have little need to spread the news in the district. Archie and his wife would see to that!

Archie eased his long, gangling frame into a cushioned chair.

"Aye, Rabbie, ye're richt there. But hae yir food first."

So in between mouthfuls of potato and potted meat, Simon's Dad told of the great and stirring scenes in Edinburgh. He told them of the huge crowds which were so dense that, as they moved along, one scarcely needed to walk because the tightly packed bodies on either side carried one along. When the leaders of the Evangelical party in the Kirk, who were opposed to the Moderates, approached St Andrew's church where the Assembly was being held, calls such as "Here comes Chalmers!" and "Here comes Candlish!" rang out. As the Queen's Commissioner to the General Assembly made his way to the church his approach was announced by the tramp of soldiers and the sound of military music.

Simon's Dad told of how different it was in the Assembly itself when Dr Welsh, the Moderator of the previous Assembly and as such the one who started the proceedings, stood up to speak. There the silence was unbearably intense. Not a foot shuffled. Not one cough broke the hushed stillness. Even throughout the reading of the long document which contained the protest of the Kirk at the way it had been treated by the courts and the government, the silence among the listeners was unbroken. But as soon as Dr Welsh rose, followed by Dr Chalmers and other leaders of the evangelicals, a loud cheer burst out from the public gallery. It soon subsided, as everyone was intent on seeing who was leaving and how many were leaving the national Kirk.

As they emerged from the church, there were shouts of "They come! They come!" A great line of ministers and elders – someone had told Simon's Dad that there had been about four hundred – made their way in a great procession to the vast Tanfield Hall in the Canonmills district of Edinburgh. Simon's Dad had great difficulty in reaching the hall because of the mass of people thronging the route and, when he reached the hall where the first Assembly of the Free Church of Scotland was held, he was disappointed to find that the hall which accommodated three thousand was packed to capacity and could hold no more.

As Simon's Dad recounted the events which rocked not only the Kirk but the nation and which created a gaping fissure in the religious landscape of Scotland, all three of his listeners, even his wife (who normally left such matters of church affairs well alone), were spellbound. The chattering Archie could only manage to interpose the occasional "Well I niver!" or "Well done" as Simon's Dad warmed to his task, forgot about his potatoes and potted meat and enjoyed holding forth to a captivated audience.

"That's very weel," said Simon's Mum. "But where are a'these ministers tae find money tae keep themselves, their wives and their weans? A' these fine principles are very well but they willnae feed ye. Hae they thocht aboot that?"

"Indeed they hae thocht aboot it, Bessie," said Simon's Dad. "Dr Chalmers has a plan by which a' the new kirks will pay intae a fund and it will then be divided among a' the ministers. It's the idea that the rich should support the poor. There are quite a few congregations in the like o' Edinburgh which are very wealthy indeed."

"Man, that's a grand idea. That Mr Chalmers must be a very clever minister," said Archie.

"He is that indeed, Archie. He's a great man. Before he was converted he wis a great mathematician. I believe it wis when

he fell ill that he wis converted. He's a grand stalwart in the cause o' Christ noo. He could easily be a Professor o' Mathematics. He wis Professor o' Systematic Theology before this Assembly an' he will continue as a professor wi' the new Kirk."

"Faither," said Simon, "where are we tae worship next Sabbath? Perhaps the laird will no allow Mr Gillespie tae preach in the kirk. And how can the folk here build a kirk? They cannae worship in fields and barns for ever."

"Well, ah dinnae richtly ken and ah'm ower tired tae think o' it after travellin' frae Edinburgh."

"Ye'll be needin' a sleep, Rabbie. Ah'll hae tae go. Thanks for the cup o' tea, Missus Shaw."

"Ye're very welcome. Gie my regards tae yir missus."

"Ah will that. Guid nicht."

"Ach, he's nae a bad soul is Archie, but they willnae need tae sell ony newspapers in this parish this week," laughed Simon's Mum.

"Ye're richt there, Bessie. We'll hae tae discuss this matter in the mornin' when ah've had a guid nicht's sleep. But first we'll hae worship. Give me that Bible, Simon."

Simon's Dad led them in worship and, as he prayed, gave thanks for the faithfulness of God in a time of upheaval and uncertainty.

DIFFICULT WORDS

Page 30	– cataclysm	*a great upheaval*
Page 32	– Queen's Commissioner	*Represent the Queen at the General Assembly*
Page 33	– fissure	*deep crack*
	– interpose	*to squeeze in*

Chapter 8

AFTER THE ECSTASY

The emotional tide which carried people along on its way of enthusiasm ebbed somewhat when the immediate excitement of what became known as the Disruption receded. Excitement was replaced with a sober realisation of the tremendous difficulties faced and an energetic determination to succeed. Simon had been elated, possibly all the more because of his father's eyewitness account of events on that decisive day in Edinburgh, but he was soon brought down to earth.

Schoolboy adherents to what became known as the Auld Kirk were scornful, vying with one another in predicting how long those who had departed from the home comforts of the mother Kirk would remain away until they came slinking back in disgrace and humiliation. They were a bunch of sheep blindly following crazy shepherds. Or donkeys, more like. Meet in a barn, would they? More like them to meet in a byre. Aye, their ministers would soon milk them. And so it went on. Simon they called Simple Simon and it was with difficulty he reminded himself that he must show self-control and dignity. Otherwise his tormentors would find even more satisfaction and know that he had been really stung. Other lads were not so restrained and some on both sides went home from school with puffed and swollen lips and bruised knucles.

※　　※　　※　　※

It was an anxious time. The Reverend Gillespie had preached his last sermon in the pulpit he had occupied for so long. He had also left a manse which, if not so grand and imposing as the one at Auchengarve, was still a handsome and comfortable house.

Now he and his wife had moved to a disused cottage more than two miles outside his parish. The laird would not lease any of the dwellings on his property and had prohibited any of his tenants from giving him lodgings. The cottage he had found was on land not owned by the Laird, who also vowed that the new church would never be able to build on one inch of his land.

The contrast between the cottage and the manse was complete. The cottage was surrounded by a wilderness of weeds which had almost obliterated the path to the front door whereas the manse had a well-kept garden, fragrant in summer with the scent of roses, honeysuckle and lilies. The manse had large, bright, airy rooms whereas the cottage had cramped, dingy rooms with damp patches on the walls. The manse had ample accommodation, an extensive library and a secluded study whereas the cottage had only a living room, a tiny kitchen and an almost equally tiny bedroom.

But what caused most anxiety to Simon and his Dad was not the situation of their minister, concerned about him though they were for he had never been robust and he was no longer a young man. Nor was it the prospect of being unable to build a church because of the implacable refusal of the Laird to grant a site. Rather it was the amount of support which they would receive from the people. It was all very well for the people to be enthusiastic when the issue was one of debate but would they be so enthusiastic when it came to taking action? It was easy to be loud in their support of evangelical leaders when they did not have to suffer anything for their principles. But when farm workers came to considering that Auld Kirk farmers might not re-employ them at the end of the farming year if they had left the Auld Kirk, would they waver and beat a retreat? Or when farmers came to considering that if they supported the new Church the laird might not renew the lease on their farms when their lease expired, would they be prepared to pay the price? Some ministers who had formerly been loud in support of the independence of the Church had grown quieter and quieter as the decisive moment had approached and had stayed in the comforts of their manses. Might not the same be true of a large number of the people? Simon and his Dad tried to comfort themselves with the thought that they should be faithful to their cause and consciences rather than expect to be successful but they could not free themselves from the niggling fear that the numbers supporting them would be derisory.

The Sunday morning dawned when the first service of the new Church or Free Church of Scotland was to be held. It was an unseasonable day. The wind from the north was sharp and the sky was overcast. The gloom made the Sabbath silence ominous. Simon's Dad had risen earlier than usual and Simon knew that he had been praying about the services. Only Simon's Mum went about her Sabbath business as usual. The house was unusually quiet.

As they took their porridge, Simon could feel the stiffness in his muscles. He and his Dad had cleared out the stackyard, erected a makeshift pulpit with trestles, an old door, a table and a chair and set out as many chairs, benches, logs and boxes as they could find. They then had spread out fresh straw in case the day turned out to be wet. Simon's Dad had worked steadily and Simon, not so used to physical work, had struggled to keep up with him.

"Simon, will ye go tae fetch Mr and Mrs Gillespie? I was goin' tae fetch him mysel but I think I had better stay here and see tae the arrangements."

Simon needed no second bidding. He loved riding on the trap. Also, it would ease the tension which he felt in the house.

"Be sure now, Simon, that ye tak care. Wrap Mrs Gillespie up well for it's nae a summer's day."

❋   ❋   ❋   ❋

On his way back with the Reverend and Mrs Gillespie Simon had to pass Mr Gillespie's former church. Mr Gillespie, who to Simon's surprise had seemed remarkably bright and talkative considering his personal circumstances and the uncertainty of the future of his congregation, had become silent as they drew near to it. Simon saw there there did not seem to be many there but he did not want to stare and seem nosey. However, out of the corner of his eye he caught sight of the Reverend Mr Ferguson, who appeared to be scowling and staring darkly in their direction.

"Was that the Reverend Ferguson at the kirk?" asked Simon.

"Yes, it was", replied Mr Gillespie simply.

"What is he doing there?" asked Simon. "He did not seem very pleased."

"He is probably there declaring the congregation vacant," said Mr Gillespie. "I dare say that he was not too pleased to see me because he is bitterly opposed to our cause and I daresay the night of the deputation when I crossed swords with him has not endeared me to him. He has avoided me since that night and when we have met he has been very cool."

"So much unpleasantness!" sighed Mrs Gillespie, a bent and

a rather melancholy woman. "It is hard on flesh and blood."

"'In this world ye shall have tribulation'," murmured Mr Gillespie, half to himself and half to his wife.

* * * *

They drove up the farm road, passing two or three people on the way, and turned into the stackyard. What a sight met their yes! The stackyard seemed to Simon to be overflowing with its great silent congregation. Barely a wisp of straw could be seen, do densely packed were the people. Simon's Dad came to help the Reverend Gillespie down but the minister made no move. All he could do was sit and stare.

Little wonder the Reverend Ferguson was thunder-faced, thought Simon to himself. When he had gone to declare the congregation vacant, little did he realise the accuracy of the expression. Not only was the pulpit vacant – the pews were too!

Having recovered from his emotion at seeing that almost the whole of his former congregation had followed him into the Free Church, Mr Gillespie entered the pulpit and started the service. To Simon, that whole service was unforgettable. The text from which Mr Gillespie preached was: 'Let us hold fast the profession of our faith without wavering; for he is faithful that promised'. Thin and tremulous though Mr Gillespie's voice was, when he read out his text his voice rang out with unusual clarity and fervency. He seemed like a man inspired as he spoke of the faithfulness of God to his promises, the danger to believers of wavering and the call for resolution among God's people. Simon was both ashamed of his own earlier timidity and anxiety and tremendously encouraged. Here was a man who impressed him not merely by his mighty words but also by his courageous example. Above all, Simon sensed there as he had never done before the presence and power of the God whose faithfulness had been so wonderfully extolled.

From that day, Simon's misty desires to be a preacher took a more definite shape and clearer definition.

DIFFICULT WORDS

Page 36	– receded	*died down*
	– elated	*in tremendously high spirits*
	– adherents	*those belonging to*
	– vying	*competing*
Page 37	– obliterated	*destroyed*
Page 38	– implacable	*unyielding*
	– expired	*ran out*
	– derisory	*laughable*
Page 40	– pews	*church bench seating*
	– tremulous	*shaky*
	– extolled	*highly praised*

Chapter 9

THUNDERBOLT

Simon stood in Mr Ferguson's study, flabbergasted and horrified.

He had entered the Auchengarve manse with his books as usual. His secret desire to become a minister had so occupied his thoughts and his mind was so intent on being successful in his studies that Mr Ferguson's black look as he drove past the previous Sunday morning had not once cast a shadow over his bright frame of mind,.

That had changed abruptly as soon as he had seen Mr Ferguson. The heavy red face was grim and ugly. The eyes were hostile. He had known instantly that Mr Ferguson was in a towering rage.

"Well, why have you come?" Mr Ferguson had demanded.

"To - to study more G-Greek," Simon had replied, stammering even more than usual.

"I know that, you blockhead! But there is more to it than that," Mr Ferguson had snapped.

Panic had seized Simon's mind. Had Mr Ferguson somehow divined that he and Annabel were fond of one another? Had Annabel tried to write him and the letter been discovered by Mr Ferguson? Had the maid been spying on them and reported seeing Simon and Annabel talking at the manse gates?

But no.

"Did I see you last Sunday morning?" Mr Ferguson had asked.

"Yes," Simon had said.

"What were you doing?"

"I was taking the Reverend Gillespie to our farm where he was to conduct public worship," Simon had replied, recovering his composure and standing his ground.

"I see," Mr Ferguson had said heavily. "Well, your father is a died-in-the-wool evangelical of the narrowest sort and no doubt you are set to follow in his footsteps. With the Free Church desperate for ministers and your father and that silver-tongued Gillespie to give you a push, no doubt you are destined to be a Free Church minister. Do not think, lad, that they will mock me. I will not be used by them for their own ends. Your Greek lessons with me are at an end. Goodbye.

Well, then, what are you standing there for? Be off with you."

Simon had begun to pull himself together and had begun to feel so annoyed that it emboldened his tongue. "I can see your point, Mr Ferguson, and I have no wish to take any advantage of you at all. You have been very kind to give me lessons and I appreciate that, but you have spoken about my father and my minister in a rather nasty way which does little credit to you. Let me remind you that it was Mr Maitland who arranged that you should tutor me, not my father and Mr Gillespie."

"BE GONE, YOU INSOLENT PUP!" roared Mr Ferguson.

Simon hastily made his way to the door, only for it to be opened by Annabel before he could reach it.

"What has happened?" she said. "I heard the shouting."

"This young upstart has taken it upon himself to lecture me", said Mr Ferguson, stabbing a finger fiercely in the direction of Simon.

"Is this true?" asked Annabel. She had turned very pale in contrast to her father whose face had turned from red to purple.

"Your father told me that he was stopping my Greek lessons and in the course of doing so made some remarks which I objected to."

Annabel stiffened. Her face flushed. Her eyes flashed. She wheeled round and opened the door. "I will show you out, Mr Shaw."

At the door, Annabel turned to face Simon. Her face was troubled and unhappy. "Simon, please forgive my father. I know it is because you have joined the Free Church that he has stopped your lessons. I wish that I was able to join your Church but it is impossible."

"Annabel, perhaps your father is right in stopping my lessons but I just hoped with that we could have parted on better terms. I enjoyed coming to the manse. Goodbye, Annabel."

"I enjoyed thinking of you here in the manse. Goodbye, Simon."

Simon trudged slowly away from the manse. Even at some distance he could hear the shouting which came from the study. Mr Ferguson was an embittered man in a foul mood. Annabel was outraged at his high-handed treatment of Simon and would give a good account of herself. It was the terrier against the bull, thought Simon and smiled to himself. He admired her pluck as much as her beauty.

Still, Simon's heart was heavy. Where would he find someone to tutor him in Greek? Would he be able to qualify for university? Mr Maitland was very friendly with Mr Ferguson and he had remained in the Auld Kirk. Would he turn against Simon and make life difficult for him? And what about Annabel? Would he ever see her again? Was his attraction to her a daft romantic notion? Was it doomed to end in failure and frustration?

DIFFICULT WORDS
Page 42   – divined   *made out or guessed*

Chapter 10

GREY HAIRS AND YOUNG SHOULDERS

Simon had been miserable after the set-to with Mr Ferguson. He sighed endlessly and moped so much that it got on his mother's nevers.

"Rabbie, we need tae dae somethin aboot Simon. He is drivin' me crazy wi' his sighin' every minute o' the day. It's mair depressin' than a wet washday."

"Aye," replied her husband, "we cannae let this go on. Ah'm goin' tae speak tae Mr Gillespie aboot him tae see if he can gie him some advice. Ah'm at a loss when it comes tae education an' university an' exams and such like."

"He's a wise man, Mr Gillespie, but has he no got his hands full at the moment?"

"He's aye got time tae speak tae someone wi' a problem. Ah' never yet heard o' him refusin' tae see someone who needed him."

❊   ❊   ❊   ❊

Simon had agreed readily to talk to Mr Gillespie. After all, he almost hero-worshipped Mr Gillespie. But where to speak to him was a problem. He did not want to have his parents hovering around. He would not feel so free to talk if they were nearby. On the other hand, the cottage where the minister stayed was so small that even if Mrs Gillespie was in the kitchen she would be bound to hear what they were saying. After some thought, Simon decided that he would go to the cottage. A minister's wife ought to know how to keep confidences and somehow the thought of the morose Mrs Gillespie overhearing him did not seem so disturbing as the thought that his Mum might hear.

46

Anyway, the gloomy little cottage seemed to fit his state of mind.

❊   ❊   ❊   ❊

"Come in, Simon. I am glad you came. You will pardon the room. It's very mixter-moxter, I'm afraid. The house is rather small for our furniture I have had to store some of it in a disused stable and I have sold one or two pieces." Simon liked the way the minister treated his come-down in housing in a matter-of-fact fashion and used the word of the people, mixter-moxter, rather than untidy.

As he busied himself tidying away some of the books he had been studying, Mrs Gillespie entered from the kitchen.

"Is that you, Simon? The kettle has just boiled and I will make a wee cup of tea."

"Thank you," said Simon, rather disappointed to find Mrs Gillspie at home as he had been hoping that Mr Gillespie might have been alone.

After they had tea, girdle scones and bramble jelly, Mrs Gillespie excused herself and said that she had someone to visit. Simon was scared that the relief in his face might show. He began to feel that he had misjudged the minister's wife. She had asked very kindly about his folks and their neighbours and had not been as withdrawn as he had expected. Perhaps she only blossomed in the confines of her own home. Perhaps he had underestimated the strain on her, not just during the upheaval of the Disruption period itself but also in the years leading up to it as it became clearer and clearer that the church and state were on a collision course.

"Well, Simon. I hear that you had a rather unpleasant visit to the Auchengarve manse."

Simon described his visit to the manse, leaving out the part that Annabel had played.

Mr Gillespie looked at Simon thoughtfully. "But did you not tell Mr Ferguson that you had no intention of going in for the ministry?"

Simon blushed. What could he say?

"So you do have thoughts of going into the ministry? Is that why you are so worried? You think that without Mr Ferguson's tutoring you will not be able to get to university and without going to university you will not be able to become a minister?"

Simon nodded.

"I see. Have you told anyone of your desire to become a minister?"

"No," said Simon.

"What made you think that you should be a minister?"

Simon told of the effect the meeting with the deputation had had on him and of how he had been thrilled when Mr Gillspie had taken the first Free Church service in the stackyard.

"Simon, becoming a minister is a solemn thing. A minister has a great responsibility for souls. I sometimes can't sleep at night when someone is on my mind. Now it is said in the Bible about the High Priest that no man takes this honour unto himself but he that is called of God. I believe that the same principle applies to ministers of the gospel. Has God called you, Simon? Or are these just your own desires? Are you being carried along on a wave of enthusiasm? There can be tough times in the ministry when the Devil does his best to leave you confused and dispirited. If you are not sure that you are called by God then it is all too easy to be ensnared."

This was not what Simon had expected. He had expected re-assurance and encouragement. Crest-fallen, he stammered, "I-I hadn't thought of it that way."

"Simon, don't think I am trying to discourage you. I would love you to be a minister of the gospel. But in the storm a ship has to have an anchor which will not drag. Now an obstacle has been placed in your way. Would you be so worried and miserable if you were convinced of your call to serve God and if you were convinced that nothing could thwart the purpose of almighty God?"

"No, Mr Gillespie." Simon felt utterly miserable. His visit to this make-shift manse was little better than his visit to the grand Auchengarve manse.

"Now, Simon, look to God to direct you. I do not know how, but I know God will direct you if your trust is in Him. Sometimes it is only as we look back that we can see that God has been guiding us. At the time it seemed as if we had been in utter darkness. God will guide you."

"Yes, Mr Gillespie," said Simon, but with little conviction.

"Perhaps you will remember that at darker times than this. Now, I have something to tell you that will really cheer you up. I will teach you Greek."

"What!" exclaimed Simon, instantly brightening up. "Why, Mr Gillespie -"

"Now, I am not nearly as good a Greek scholar as Mr Ferguson, but I know my New Testament Greek very well and did well enough at Classical Greek as a student. If we both work hard you will get through." Mr Gillespie smoothed back his thin grey hair and his bony features lit up with a smile.

"That's wonderful. I cannae thank ye enough." In his excitement, Simon had lapsed back into his native Scots."

"Dinnae try," said Mr Gillespie, laughing as he responded in Scots himself. "But there are two things I want to say before you rush home to your books. The first is that there are many ways that you can serve God outside the ministry. For example, the Free Church has decided that it is going to build its own schools. There are many teachers who have lost their posts because they have joined the Free Church. I have heard it said that as many as six hundred and fifty teachers have been dismissed. However, I am convinced that in a few years there will be a great need for teachers. The new church has lost no time in trying to raise funds for building schools. I remember, too, hearing Dr Duff of Calcutta in India speaking at the Assembly – in 1836 if my memory serve me correctly – of his work in India and the great opportunities there for the gospel. He held us all spellbound. He is a great teacher and a great speaker. You never know, Simon, you might be another Dr Duff."

Simon blushed.

"Now the other thing is that you must not think too harshly of Mr Ferguson. He has never been the same man since his wife died. He is a real Moderate, of course, and has taken the Disruption badly, but for all that he is a gentleman."

"Thanks, Mr Gillespie. You've given me a lot to think about. I'm sorry to have taken up your time. You can get back to your books now."

"Aye, Simon, I'll need to do that to polish up my Greek!" joked Mr Gillespie. "Give me regards to your parents."

"I will, Mr Gillespie," said Simon. "Thanks again."

"Goodbye, Simon." Mr Gillespie looked fondly after Simon. Yes, Simon was impressionable. But his heart was in the right place and, after all, you couldn't put an old head on young shoulders. He just hoped that he hadn't been too hard on young Simon.

DIFFICULT WORDS
Page 46 – morose   *gloomy*

Chapter 11

FAREWELLS

Simon swung up into the trap feeling awkward and embarrassed. He wished that he could have slipped away quietly with no fuss. He admired his mother. She was a no-nonsense person herself and always avoided the limelight. She knew how he felt and though she might shed a few tears after he had gone and when no-one would see her, there would be no tearful partings.

His father had insisted in taking him to Edinburgh, even though there was plenty to do in the fields and Simon would have been as happy going by the public coach. Simon wondered if it was because his Dad was an emotional man. Already his voice was gruff and husky. It would be easier for him to say goodbye to Simon alone in Edinburgh.

It was really the presence of the neighbours and Mr Gillespie which most embarrassed him. It was as if this was an official send-off, something like the launch of a new ship. What if he failed miserably to cope with university? How embarrassing if the newly launched ship sprang a leak and slowly sank within sight of the slipway!

"Aye, lad, ye'll need tae watch those bold hussies in Edinburgh,' said squint-eyed Archie. "Ane o' them cam up tae me when ah was still a good-lookin' young man an' put her airm roond me. 'Tak yir airm aff o' me,' I said, 'or ah'll hae ye clapped in irons.' Ye couldnae see her for stoor."

"A likely story!" scoffed his wife and added, among general laughter, "Ye were niver good-lookin'!"

"That's nae whit ye said the nicht I proposed," countered Archie, raisin' more laughter and adding to Simon's discomfiture.

51

"Simon's nae daft" said Mrs Scott, another neighbour.

"Does that mean ah am? quipped Archie.

"Well, put it this way: if ye were in Edinburgh, ah doubt it wisnae tae study at the university", retorted Mrs Scott.

Even Archie, in irrepressible mood, had no answer to the perfect put-down. Mr Gillespie saw his opportunity. "Archie is quite right, you know, to warn against Edinburgh with its temptations. But I am not here to preach a sermon. Simon, it has been a great pleasure to see you grow up to be a credit to your parents and I am sure that you will continue to make them proud of you. We all wish you every success in your studies. Now we shall bow our heads as I commit Simon to the Lord in prayer." Mr Gillespie prayed briefly but warmly for Simon.

"God bless ye, Simon. Take care o' yirsel," said his Mum simply. His Dad flicked the reins, the mare trotted off and, as Simon waved and waved, a lump formed in his throat.

When they had reached the end of the farm road in silence. Simon's Dad said, "It was guid o' Mr Maitland tae call last nicht.

Ah'm sure that he would hae been there tae see ye on yir road had he no tae be at the Academy."

"He's a very fair man, Mr Maitland. Ah thocht he micht hae had a spite at me because we left the Kirk but he treated each pupil the same whether they were Auld Kirk or Free Kirk. Mind ye, he still puts the fear o' death in me."

"Aye, ye niver lose that fear o' a schoolmaster ye've had yirsel."

❋　　❋　　❋　　❋

Two miles along the road, Simon and his dad met a trap going in the opposite direction. As they drew near one another, the other trap seemed to slow down. Suddenly, Simon's heart gave a leap. It was Annabel!

"Slow down, Faither," whispered Simon.

"Whit for, lad? Are ye all richt?"

"I'm fine, Faither."

"Simon!" called Annabel. "Simon, it's been a while since I've seen you."

Simon was at a loss for words. "Annabel, I-I Annabel, this is my father. Father, this is Miss Annabel Ferguson."

"Pleased to meet you, Mr Shaw," said Annabel with a graceful nod of her head.

"And you, Miss Ferguson. I take it that your father is minister at Auchengrave. I hope he is well."

"He was not too well after the great exodus of ministers from the Church of Scotland to form the Free Church but he is more like himself now."

After his first excitement at seeing Annabel, Simon was now feeling distinctly uncomfortable and talk about Mr Ferguson did nothing to improve it.

"Annabel, I am on my way to Edinburgh. I am going ot university."

"I know," said Annabel.

"You know?" said Simon, taken aback. "How did you find

out?"

"Oh, I have ways and means," said Annabel coyly. "My father says that determination is my middle name. Anyway, I just want to wish you well in your studies. I will pray for you. Goodbye, Simon. Goodbye, Mr Shaw."

"Thank you, Annabel. I will pray for you too. Goodbye."

"Ye're a richt dark horse, Simon Shaw," said his Dad when they were out of sight. "She must be richt keen on ye afore she would be oot watchin' for ye going off."

"Och, Faither, she feels sorry for the way her faither made a scene and ordered me oot o' the manse. That's why she wanted tae wish me well."

"Oh, aye," said his Dad sceptically and chuckled to himself.

Simon was silent and gazed out onto the fields, seemingly absorbed in the fascinating spectacle of the stubble in the reaped fields beginning to blacken after the autumn rains.

Chapter 12

AULD REEKIE

Edinburgh overwhelmed Simon at first. The shouts of fishwives and hawkers and the din of harnesses creaking and hooves clattering on cobbled streets assaulted his ears. The smell of garbage and foul drains, only partially disguised by the smell of the smoke which gave Edinburgh its nickname 'Auld Reekie', offended his nostrils. He was shocked by the crime and by the poverty and filth of some of the back streets. In contrast, he gazed in wonder and admiration at the noble buildings – the grimly brooding castle, the distinctive crown-topped architecture of St Giles', the regal impressiveness of Holyroodhouse Palace and the superb elegance of the great terraces of the New Town. Hearing about them was one thing, seeing them was quite another.

The university overwhelmed him at first, too. The Professor of Humanity not only taught Latin but spoke in it when scolding the students, something he did frequently and with terrible displays of temper. Normally, he was as aloof and distant as the Greek gods of Mount Olympus who featured in the ancient Greek literature which he taught. Simon hated catching the gaze of his icy, glittering eyes. How different was the mathematical class! The lecturer was utterly eccentric and absent-minded. His darting eyes, jerking movements like those produced by an inexpert puppeteer and gabbling voice all made him an object of derision. His explanations were hasty, his figures crammed together in an incomprehensible jumble and his geometrical drawings scrappy. No sooner had he finished a rapid and garbled explanation of some geometric figure which he had chalked on a board than he would vigorously rub it off, creating a small cloud

55

of dust sufficient occasionally to make him cough. From this habit and the dryness of his subject arose his nickname. 'Dr Dust'. More than once, 'Dr Dust' delivered lectures he had already given the previous day. Simon was filled with a terror of failing to understand one particle of the mathematics course. Night by night he agonised over what he was going to do. Should he speak to the lecturer? Should he write to Mr Maitland for advice? Should he just give up? His problem was solved by one of his fellow students.

"You're looking terribly glum, Simon. What's happened? Has your landlady thrown you out? Any bad news from home?"

"Nothing like that. I'm just worried about the mathematics class. I just can't follow it. I'll never pass an exam in it."

"Nonsense, Simon. All you need is a copy of old Dr Dust's lectures. He had them published. Everyone just gets them. I study his book but I only go to the lectures to be entertained by his antics."

Simon's landlord was a peppery little man who tolerated fools not at all. A watchmaker, Thomas Bain was most fussy about punctuality. If breakfast was served at seven o'clock, it was most definitely not served at five past seven. Simon once, and only once, made the mistake of complaining. If he was in awe of Edinburgh itself and of the university, he was petrified of his landlord. One sight of his pale round face, perpetual frown and neat little black moustache curled down at the edges was enough to tighten up his muscles and bring back the stutter which had almost gone for good. His lodgings were up a close in the historic High Street. It was little more than a garret up five flights of foot-worn steps with no heating other than that given off by a smoky oil lamp. How often he lay on the lumpy horse-hair mattress pulling the bedclothes – to which he had added his overcoat and jacket in a vain attempt to keep himself warm – over himself and allowing his mind to wander to his folks cosy in their well-warmed farm house. How he longed for the welcoming blaze of a log fire and the continual heat radiating from the old black range in the kitchen. He dreamed, too, of the open fields, of the smell of the freshly ploughed earth, of the lowing of cattle and the steam rising from the horses' backs. Sometimes, too, he dreamed of Annabel. Why had she come to see him off? Was his mother right in thinking that Annabel was not destined for the likes of him and that the sooner he rid himself of daft romantic notions the better?

The Sabbath was often a welcome relief from the eye-straining business of studying. Free Churches had been built with astonishing speed: in one year after the Disruption 470 churches had been built, all being paid for by the generous and enthusiastic giving of the people. This phenomenal number was not maintained, one reason being the stubborn refusal of land-owners in many parts of the country to give land for churches because of their opposition to the Free Church. Simon often thought of his own parents worshipping in a barn when he went to the large, comfortble if mostly plain churches recently built in the capital city.

Being a student, Simon took advantage of that to go to different churches and hear the best preachers of the day. He loved to write to his father, telling him that he had been to hear such-and-such a preacher in such-and-such a church and what the text had been. The preacher's manner and appearance were described, but always the main headings of the sermon were given pride of place along with any helpful illustrations or quoteworthy sayings. His father had written him once express-ing pleasure at being kept so well informed of the church activities and ministers of the capital but warning him of the dangers of being a mere sermon taster going out of curiosity to hear famous preachers rather than going with a spiritual hunger to hear the Word of the Lord.

He often heard Dr Gordon of the Free High Church, Dr Bruce of Free St Andrew's, Dr Candlish of Free St. George's and Dr Guthrie of Free St John's. He was impressed by the gracious character, cultured bearing and quiet dedication of Dr John

Wilson of Bombay, whom he heard speak once. Dr Wilson had heard of the Disruption in Egypt on his way home from India. Without delay, he had resigned his position on the mission field and joined the Free Church. Not only the house he had built in Bombay with the help of the generosity of friends, but also his library and scientific equipment purchased with private donations had been demanded by the Church of Scotland and handed over. Despite the impression made on Simon by the missionary, time and his studies conspired to make it only a temporary impression. He heard all of the Professors at New College which was held in George Street, then, before the imposing college building was erected at the top of the Mound. He loved the eccentric but brilliant Dr John Duncan, known as 'Rabbi' Duncan because of his learning and knowledge of the Jews and their history. Simon always sensed that Dr Duncan felt that he was on holy ground in preaching the gospel.

One incident in his early days in Edinburgh struck him as strange. He had been walking home rather absent-mindedly, his head in the clouds, when a snarling of dogs, a frenzied whinnying and a piercing scream jerked him out of his reverie. He whirled round to see a young horse rearing and backing as three dogs which had burst out of a side close rolled over in a whirl of yelps, growls, bared fangs and flailing paws. The young lady in the trap behind the horse had no control of it as the trap had been backed into barrels arranged outside a wine merchant's shop and was beginning to topple precariously. Just then a young man in a claret coloured coat with brass buttons rushed out of the shop, launched himself over a toppled barrel and grabbed at the horse's harness. Immediately, Simon, who had stood frozen to the spot till that moment, leapt into action. He dashed over, jumped on the foot-step and whisked the lady down in one sweeping movement.

To his dismay, the lady was not at all grateful. "Let me down, I say. Unhand me at once. I demand," she said quite aggressively. Simon let her down gently and withdrew his hand from round her waist.

"How shall I live this down? It's all that fool Robert's fault. Frightened out of my wits, rescued by a clownish Scottish Sir Galahad, no doubt having to go home to Papa with a broken carriage and probably being late for dinner – what an afternoon! How I hate this city!" she wailed in her posh English accent.

Simon stood silent and crimson-faced as she vented her frustration.

"Ye should hae left her tae cope intae the gutters. Perhaps it wid hae knocked some sense intae tht giddy head o' hers," growled a voice at Simon's ear.

The man in the claret coat eventually calmed down the horse and called to the lady. "Miss Amelia, I hope you did not receive too much of a fright."

"I am as well as can be expected in such distressing circumstances," she replied coldly. "Please take me home."

She turned to Simon and tilted her head to one side. She was uncommonly pretty, but though a smile played round her mouth, it was a smile of amused condescension. "Perhaps the young Sir Galahad would help me up?"

"Why, y-yes, ma'am," stuttered Simon foolishly and held her arm as she ascended.

Neither she nor the man in the claret coat uttered a word of thanks or gave a backward glance as they set off.

"Bah!" spat the man who had growled his displeasure earlier. "Ye're a daft gowk. Ah'd see myself swing afore ah'd gie her a civil word. An' they ca' themselves gentry," he said mockingly.

The small crowd which had gathered, as they always do when some disturbance occurs, dispersed and Simon made his way to his lodgings. Later that night he reflected on the similarity between the episode that day and that which had occurred years before. Both has involved a pony and trap. In both a horse or pony had received a freight and endangered a young lady in the trap. In both he had rescued a beautiful young lady. But there the resemblance ended. Annabel had grace and wit and charm;

Amelia had only a haughty beauty. Annabel had never forgotten what Simon had done for her whereas Amelia had sneered and had humiliated him. Despite the trouble caused by the ruined eggs, Simon had felt a secret satisfaction in doing what he would never have believed himself capable of beforehand when he had rescued Annabel; that day's episode had left him dismayed and disgusted at his treatment. Edinburgh had never seemed so mean a place. Annabel seemed even more attractive in her personality than ever. Simon longed to be out of the bewildering city and to be home with the people he loved and the way of life he knew.

DIFFICULT WORDS
Page 55   – regal   *kingly or queenly*
          – aloof   *feeling superior and different*
          – Mount   *a mountain in Greece which was*
            Olympus   *supposed to be the home of the god*
          – derision   *scorn*

	– garbled	*in confusing bits and pieces*
Page 56	– petrified	*terrified (turned to stone with fear)*
	– perpetual	*continual*
	– garret	*a room just under the roof*
Page 57	– phenomenal	*remarkable*
	– cultured bearing	*well-bred way of conducting oneself*
Page 58	– conspired	*worked together*
	– imposing	*impressive*
	– reverie	*daydream*
	– precariously	*insecurely and dangerously*
Page 59	– Sir Galahad	*a gallant knight in the tales of King Arthur*
	– condescension	*lowering oneself to talk to an inferior person*

Chapter 13

AT THE CHALK FACE

Nearly three years later Simon found himself walking to the newly formed Free Church school in his native parish.

The old Laird had taken a stroke and died. True to his word, not an inch of his land had been granted to the Free Church in his lifetime. But his nephew who had inherited the estate had adopted the view that the Free Church had come to stay and there was little point in postponing the inevitable. Besides, the income from the sale would not go wrong! He had granted sites for a church, a manse and a school on sites which were agriculturally worthless and which were far from ideally situated. But the Free Church had been in no position to drive a hard bargain and, despite some haggling, had been glad to have the security of its own sites and buildings.

Simon had abandoned the idea of becoming a minister, for the time being anyway. He came to see that Mr Gillespie's questioning had indeed exposed the truth: he had been carried away by the current of feeling at the time. Not wanting to be stranded on some barren shore when the current slackened, he had turned his mind to teaching. Now, as he made his way to the school to start teaching there for the first time, doubts began to creep into his mind. Had he merely exchanged one enthusiasm for another? Certainly, there had been a tremendous vision and burst of enthusiasm in the new church for education, not lessened in any way by the dismissal of hundreds of teachers throughout Scotland for belonging to the Free Church. Great sums of money had been raised among the people at a time when the demands upon people's generosity were great due to the church and manse building programme. Would he be able to teach effectively? Would he be respected as the local lad made good or would it be the case that a prophet is not without honour except in his own corner? Was it timidity and a parochial outlook which had led him back to his home parish or was it in the providence of God that the Free Church school was opening at this point in his life?

❋   ❋   ❋   ❋

Some few months later, Simon was still troubled, but not by the doubts of that first day. He had enjoyed teaching, hard work though it had been. His country background and his knowledge of the parents had, he thought, been a great asset. He had introduced new idea such as nature study and the country children loved it. Though he had set out to model himself on Mr Maitland and be strict but fair, he rarely had to punish a pupil.

What troubled and angered him were the rumours and innuendos. He heard that he was being accused of poisoning the minds of the children against the Auld Kirk and telling false stories to blacken the names of the Auld Kirk ministers. He was nothing but an upstart, some folks said, and all that traipsing about field and ponds was just a big waste of time when he should be drumming in spelling and teaching them sums.

The most galling thing to Simon was that he could not pin down the rumours, nor even decide if what Auld Kirk people had said about him had been exaggerated by Free Kirk people. People, especially country people, being what they were, this was more than likely the case. But even if he had identified the culprits, what good would that have done? All he could do was deny the rumours, not disprove them. The best thing, he decided, was to say nothing and hope that the results of his teaching would speak for themselves.

After all, at that time jibes and counter-jibes were rife. Didn't the little ditty sum it all up?

> The wee kirk, the Free Kirk,
> The kirk wi'oot the steeple;

> *The Auld Kirk, the cauld kirk,*
> *The kirk wi' oot the people.*

Local rhymsters were more personal:

> *Gillespie is an auld galoot*
> *Wha bid his people a' come oot.*
> *'I've lost my stipend,' he did say.*
> *'Now a' you folk hae got tae pay.'*

To this the Free Kirk rhymster had rather weakly responded:

> *Auld Ferguson is scared tae death.*
> *Whit's wrang, ye Auld Kirk hero?*
> *In kirk he's haunted by his words*
> *Which aye come back an echo.*

His anxiety over the unseemly strife and ill-feeling was allayed by the person he least expected: Mr Maitland. Mr Maitland was about to retire and Simon went to his house to wish him well in his retirement and give him a book as a token of appreciation for the encouragement Mr Maitland had given him. Mr Maitland had enquired about his progress and before Simon knew it he was telling this austere schoolmasterly figure of the slanders passed around about him and the prejudices against some of his ways.

"Don't you listen to their stuff and nonsense", barked Mr Maitland as if he were talking to an erring schoolboy. "Clattering tongues in empty heads, that's what they are," he fumed, his white whiskers bristling furiously. "If there is one thing I cannot stand it is petty-minded people. Now I disagreed with those who went out of the national Kirk. I think they had a point but they could have compromised. However, I admire them for sticking to their principles. I tell you I was wild when I learned that James Ferguson had stopped your Greek lessons. I told him that it was as well we were not in the Free Kirk because if we were I would not have contributed a penny towards his stipend. Did I tell you that before?"

"No, sir. But I would have liked to have seen Mr Ferguson's face when you said it."

"You're right, it was a sight to see," grunted Mr Maitland. "His face went through more changes of colour than a chameleon's body. I don't suppose he was used to being crossed like that. I didn't mince my words in school, as you well know, and I was never in the habit of doing it outside school either."

"I can vouch for the fact that you spoke what was on your mind in school all right. But talking of that, I know that you were interested in the Ancient Picts. Now I have a book here which I hope might be of interest to you. It is called "Ancient Picts and Ancient Romans". I hope you don't have the book already."

"No, Simon, I don't. Now that is really good of you. It's strange that you should give me this book. I was just thinking of my retirement and vowing to myself that I was not going to spend it in vacant idleness. I had formed the idea of giving a series of lectures next winter on topics which I think might be of general educational interest and this was one of the topics I was turning over in my mind. You couldn't have made a better choice."

Simon felt very pleased at himself. It had been in inspired choice prompted by casually scanning the reviews in an Edinburgh magazine. Mr Maitland's pleasure had set the seal on a very pleasant visit. He would not forget the evening in a hurry. And indeed, whenever he heard of the rumours and jibes, Mr Maitland's bristling whiskers came into his mind's eye and he imagined that he could almost hear again Mr Maitland growling the words, "Clattering tongues in empty heads". And then, dismissing the rumours and jibes, he would smile to himself.

DIFFICULT WORDS

Page 62	– haggling	*hard bargaining*
Page 63	– innuendos	*sly hinting*
	– jibes	*scoffing or hurtful remarks*
	– rife	*extremely common*
Page 64	– allayed	*lessened*
	– austere	*stern*

Chapter 14

MUTUAL INTEREST

It was the evening of Mr Maitland's first lecture. After a fine October day, darkness had descended and the night air had become cold with the suggestion of a touch of frost before morning. Mr Maitland had hired the hall in Millerton Academy where he had so often led the school assembly and in these familiar surroundings was to deliver a lecture on 'The Ancient Picts', the first of a series called 'Peoples of the Past'. A sizeable number of people had gathered from the surrounding district, many of them former pupils of Mr Maitland.

Simon had recognised quite a few in the audience: Dr Johnston, or Dr Snuff as he was popularly known from his proverbial fondness for snuff; Andrew Lang, the tailor in Millerton, who was notorious as an atheist and radical; William Erskine, the grain merchant, or Barley Bill as he was nicknamed; Mr Logie, one of his former teachers, who was familiarly known as Walnut because of his wrinkled, swarthy skin; and some farmers whom he had met when he had been taken by his Dad to cattle sales and the like during holidays.

Simon had sat near the back. He liked sitting at the back as he could see all that was going on and who were there. His hearing was good so he had no need like some of the more timeworn members of the audience to sit at the front. Besides, retired or not, Mr Maitland had a voice which could be heard outside the hall, far less at the back.

Suddenly, Simon sat up. There, coming into the hall, was Annabel. He had not seen her since the day he had left home for Edinburgh. Who was with her? It was a slightly older woman whom Simon did not know. Annabel looked as graceful as ever.

66

Mr Maitland mounted the platform, a little brown case in one hand and a large rolled-up map tucked under the other arm. He pinned up the map rather ostentatiously. Then he opened the case, took out his notes and shook them. After surveying his audience severely, he started.

"Welcome to this series of lectures, ladies and gentlemen. I am pleased to see a number of the fairer sex here. I know that not everyone agrees, but in my view it has been a great mistake for us to have neglected educating young girls. However, I must not digress.

I would like also to thank the trustees of the Academy for granting permission to use this fine hall.

My subject tonight is 'The Ancient Picts'. I am very much indebted to a former pupil, Mr Simon Shaw, for a book which he gave to me when I retired and which has been a great help to me in the preparation of this lecture."

Simon was startled at the unexpected mention of his name. One or two heads turned in his direction but he noted with a tinge of disappointment that Annabel remained stock still. However, he turned his attention to Mr Maitland's lecture and was soon engrossed in it. Mr Maitland was obviously enjoying having such an attentive audience and pronounced his views on matters of scholarly debate with characteristic bluntness and authority.

At the end of the lecture he saw Annabel look slowly round the hall. As he made his way out, Annabel and her companion were making their exit at the same time.

"Oh, Mr Shaw," said Annabel, "I haven't seen you for ages. This is my cousin Elizabeth. Elizabeth, this is Mr Shaw whom Mr Maitland referred to at the beginning of his lecture.

"Pleased to meet you, Madam," said Simon, politely. "Did you enjoy the lecture?"

"I'm afraid not," laughed Annabel. "She kept stifling yawns. Elizabeth is not really interested. She only came because my father thought I needed an escort."

"Annabel, you are dreadful," giggled Elizabeth, but she did not deny the truth of what Annabel had said.

Simon saw his opportunity. Well, I would be very pleased to escort you to the next lecture, Miss Fergsuon. That would spare your cousin a few yawns."

Elizabeth giggled again. "Why, ye-" started Annabel, but checked herself before the words came out and bit her lip. "Thank you for your offer, Mr Shaw but I am afraid I cannot accept. It would not do for a strange man to be my chaperone."

"But -"

"You will excuse us now, Mr Shaw. My father might be getting anxious about us. Goodnight, Mr Shaw."

"Goodnight, Miss Ferguson. Goodnight Miss Elizabeth. I hope you enjoy the company of Miss Ferguson and her father."

As Annabel hustled her cousin out of the hall, Simon was dismayed. Why had Annabel taken cold feet? Had someone been overhearing the conversation? Had Annabel already been promised to some young man of means? Was it that her cousin would tell all about Simon and Annabel was afraid that her father would put his foot down? Was it that she would not tell her father yet would not go behind his back?

That night Simon felt like the legendary Tantalus punished by having a tree with clusters of fruit on it just out of reach above his head and plunged up to his chin in a river of Hades which receded every time he tried to drink it. How near he had been to Annabel and how near she had been to accepting his invitation!

※   ※   ※   ※

That night when he reached home the talk was of the lecture.

"Ah ken fine ah widnae hae understood a word o' it," commented his Mum. "Ah suppose it wis a' the gentry an' educated folks that were there."

"Aye, ah suppose maist o' them were. But there were some fairmers there whose faces ah kent well enough. Ah thought Mr

Ferguson of the Auld Kirk wid hae been there. He wis always friendly wi' Mr Maitland."

"No sae much since the Disruption, Simon. Things have cooled aff between them."

"Whit aboot his dochter? Dae ye ever see her, faither?"

"Aye, ah see her every market day. She goes aboot visitin' in a pony an' trap. Folks say she's a good soul an' verra kind tae puir souls in need. Dae ye ever see her yersel?" he asked slyly.

"She wis at Mr Maitland's lecture," replied Simon in a very matter-of fact voice.

"Hmph," snorted his Mum. "Easily seen she wis born tae marry gentry and nae tae hae tae slave ower a stove all day and darn all night."

"Talkin' o' work, ah hae tae write a report for the district inspector. Ah'd better get on wi' it."

"We'll hae family worship first, Simon."

Simon fetched the family Bible which his father always read. Simon was asked to open in prayer. This he did, asking a blessing on their worship. Then they sang four verses of a psalm and Simon's Dad read a chapter from the Bible. Finally, Simon's Dad prayed, giving thanks for the blessings of the day but especially for Christ and his atoning sacrifice and asking for continued mercy, provision, guidance and protection. The Church of Christ was prayed for, as were all loved onces and those who were strangers to the grace of God. Simon's father never prayed long, yet his simple prayers could be very moving because they came from the heart.

After saying his goodnights. Simon trudged off to his room.

"You mark ma words", said Simon's Dad. "That boy is keen on the lassie Fergsuon or ma name's nae Shaw."

"Weel, if that is so, mark ma words: Miss Ferguson's faither will maist certainly no be keen on his dochter showin' interest in a Free Kirk schoolteacher frae a far frae wealthy background."

DIFFICULT WORDS

Page 66	– notorious	*publicly known (in a bad sense)*
Page 67	– ostentatiously	*proudly showing off*
Page 68	– chaperone	*one who accompanies a lady for safety etc.*

Chapter 15

A FRIENDSHIP BLOSSOMS

Simon's Dad had inadvertently given the information that Simon had wanted. During holidays he could arrange to meet Annabel 'accidentally'. Surely her cousin would not be going round helping the poor.

Meanwhile, he continued to go the lectures over the winter months. Always Annabel would be there. Most times he would be able to say a few words to her. Despite her outward reserve, he believed that the look in her eye betrayed deeper feelings.

As things worked out, Simon did not have to wait long to meet Annabel in a different situation. This time Simon had been asked to speak at the newly-formed Ladies Mutual Improvement Society. This had been the brainchild of Mrs Carruthers, the widow of a wealthy merchant. Her house was the meeting place for the society. She was a formidable woman whom would be crossed by no-one. The subject Simon had been asked to speak on was '*The Uses of Poetry*'.

Who on earth would have thought of him? He had no contact with Mrs Carruthers or her group of women. Suddenly, it dawned on him – Mr Maitland. Mr Maitland and Mrs Curruthers were on good terms, though they sparred verbally with one another too.

At first Simon could make little of his subject. Poetry, surely, was not a practical matter to be judged by its usefulness. But gradually he worked out what he saw as roles for poetry: to "soothe a savage breast" just as David's harp had soothed the disturbed moods of King Saul, to form a memorable and therefore useful form of instruction, to express beautiful thoughts and to rouse emotions when the clarion call of the trumpet is needed.

71

He spent much time reading poetry and trying to find the most suitable poems to illustrate the points he was making. It was with considerable nervousness that he thought of the talk, never having spoken to any group of adults before on any subject. The thought of Mrs Carruthers in particular made his knees feel weak. Why had he foolishly agreed?

❈   ❈   ❈   ❈

He sat in the spacious chintz chair with elaborately carved legs feeling dwarfed by his surroundings. Had he ever been in such lavish surroundings before? What had he in common with these aristocratic-looking women some of whom even wore their advancing years with elegance? Wasn't he the son of a small-time farmer with a thick accent and roughened hands? He had stuttered when he had introduced himself to Mrs Carruthers, a fault which he had thought his student days had cured.

In walked Annabel. Almost all the women had taken their seats. She walked serenely, smiled graciously to her neighbour and sat down with a poise which, even in that well-bred company, was worthy of note. At first taken aback by her unexpected appearance, Simon then determined that he was not going to let himself down by mumbling and stuttering his way through his talk.

And neither he did. He surprised himself by the confidence he showed once he had warmed to his theme. He had even begun to enjoy himself. He handled the questions at the end with ease and when Mrs Carruthers rose up at the end she was genuinely complimentary.

"I must confess to you, ladies, that I was rather dubious when Mr Maitland suggested that we asked our friend Mr Shaw to speak to us. However, I respect Mr Maitland's judgement in most things and especially in respect of character. Therefore I proceeded to invite Mr Shaw who quite unnecessarily belittled himself and who agreed only reluctantly to come. I am glad that I paid heed to Mr Maitland's advice and no heed to Mr Shaw's protestations of inability." The ladies' faces lit up with amusement. "Mr Shaw convinced us not only of the usefulness of poetry, but also its beauty. Indeed, I felt that he became so involved in his subject and waxed so eloquent that he himself became quite poetical. It was a pleasure to listen to you, Mr Shaw, and we can rest assured that the education of the children in your school is in good hands. I propose a vote of thanks to Mr Shaw."

Afterwards, Simon manged to emerge from the house alongside Annabel.

"Do you have an escort, Miss Ferguson? I would gladly escort you home."

"That is very kind of you, Mr Shaw. I have no escort as it is only a short distance to the manse."

When out of earshot, Annabel said, "I was most impressed with you Simon. I had no idea you were such a literary scholar."

Simon laughed, "I'm no scholar. But I must admit that I enjoy poetry. Perhaps it rubbed off on me from Mr Maitland. He can quote verse upon verse upon verse. I've learned some too. Here's a sample. It's a sixteenth century song I came across.

> *In pride of May*
> *The fields are gay,*
> *The birds do sweetly sing*
> *So nature would*
> *That all things should*
> *With joy begin the Spring*
>
> *Then, Lady dear*
> *Do you appear*
> *In beauty like the Spring.*
> *I dare well say*
> *The birds that day*
> *More cheerfully will sing.*

Do you like it?"

Annabel stopped. She looked Simon straight in the eye.

"Simon, are you trying to tell me something?"

"Annabel, I don't know how to say this other than to come straight out with it. I love you."

"Simon, I don't quite know what to say. You know that I have always been fond of you."

"I know that. But I didn't know how you were placed. You could have been become friendly with another man while I was in Edinburgh. You seemed very formal when I spoke to you at Mr Maitland's lectures."

"I had my cousin with me. I did not want to do anything which might upset my father. Besides, you might have rescued some other damsel in distress in Edinburgh and have forgotten about me."

"In fact I did rescue a damsel in Edinburgh. You'll soon start thinking that I make a habit of it,' he said teasingly. "But I couldn't rescue her from herself."

"What do you mean? You're talking in riddles. Is that all the good university did you? You were just a simple country boy when we first met."

"Less of the simple," growled Simon. She had touched a sensitive spot. He apologised and then told her of the jibes he had experienced at the time of the Disruption. This led on, to how he had experienced a snide whispering campaign against him when he first started teaching in the Free Kirk school.

"But enough about that." Simon then explained about his rescue of Amelia and her treatment of him. "So, you see, I was in no danger of forgetting you. Neither Amelia or all the lassies of Edinburgh would be able to achieve that." Simon then went on to tell of the advice given by Archie as Simon was about to leave for university and of how Mrs Scott had put him in his place. They had a good laugh about it.

"Oh, Simon," said Annabel, "my father will be wondering what has happened to me. I must go."

"Annabel, we will meet again. I really enjoyed our talk. Remember what I said to you."

"Good-bye, Simon. We will meet gain."

✳   ✳   ✳   ✳

They did meet again, but not openly. They had time to talk and share their experiences as Christians, their views on books they had read, the influences in their live, their experiences of home life and their views on the issues of the day. They felt they had really begun to know one another. Their relationship flowered rapidly, like a seemingly barren landscape in an arid climate which, when it receives a rare deluge, turns almost overnight into a sea of flowers. Was it possible that others did not notice the sparkle in Annabel"s brown eyes and the bloom on her cheeks?

✳   ✳   ✳   ✳

Spring merged into the long warm days of summer and summer gradually gave way to the russet tints and colder nights of autumn. Most of the leaves had fallen when Simon decided that he must take the bull by the horns. Their relationship had to come out into the open. Despite Annabel's misgivings, he had to speak to her father.

DIFFICULT WORDS

Page 71	– inadvertently	*without intending to*
Page 72	– chintz	*a printed cotton material*
	– aristocratic	*lord-like (lady-like)*
	– belittled	*made to appear worthless*
Page 73	– protestations	*determined declarations*
Page 74	– snide	*mean and sneering*

Chapter 16

A WITHERING BLAST

The spring in Simon's foot when he left home had gone as Simon trudged up the driveway to the manse. He had written asking for an interview with Mr Ferguson on a personal matter and had received a reply stating a date and time. Now, as he looked up the avenue of bare-branched trees, he was filled with gloomy foreboding and his heart sank.

He rang the bell and was ushered in by the same round-faced maid. Not an article of furniture had altered in the manse. Time seemed to have stood still.

"Well, Mr Shaw, I seem to know your face."

"You used to give me Greek lessons, Mr Ferguson."

"Oh – I remember now. I should have known – Braeside Farm. Well, what can I do for you? Your letter referred to a 'personal matter' which wasn't exactly explicit," said Mr Ferguson coldly.

Simon gulped and thought to himself: there's no turning back. "The – the matter is personal but it concerns us both. You may not have been totally aware of it but I have been talking to your daughter at the lectures Mr Maitland has been giving in Millerton Academy. I also met her when I was asked to address The Ladies' Mutual Improvement Society. We have also conversed at other times."

"What! Totally aware! I had not the slightest indication that you were seeing my daughter. I want to see Annabel about this." He stomped to the door and shouted, "Annabel! Come here! I want to see you."

Oh dear, thought Simon, this is not going well.

Annabel entered, a strained, tense look on her features.

"Annabel, this gentleman tells me that he has been talking to you at the lectures and at other times. It is obvious that these talks went far beyond mere polite conversation."

"Yes, that is correct."

"You did not tell me that you were seeing Mr Shaw. You knew very well that I would be displeased that you were seeing Mr Shaw."

Annabel shrugged her shoulders and looked him in the eye. "I did not expect your approval and therefore I did not tell you. You were vindictive to Mr Shaw once before and treated him harshly. That might have been understandable in the heat of the controversy when the church split, though it still wasn't fair. Mr Shaw once saved me when my pony bolted. I, however, did not really know him. The only way to get to know him was to meet him and talk to him. Had I found him an honourable and attractive person, I thought you might be more favourably disposed towards him."

"There is more to this than meets the eye," growled Mr Ferguson. "What is your concern for the ill-done-by Mr Shaw?"

"Mr Ferguson," interrupted Simon, believing that now he had to grasp the nettle, "as far as I am concerned the past is the past. I have always admired your daughter for her beauty, her intelligence, her lively mind and her Christian character. In these past months we have grown very fond of one another. In short, I wish to marry your daughter and to ask permission to have your daughter's hand in marriage."

"Permisson? Marriage? Over my dead body!" exploded Mr Ferguson. "What infernal impudence! You base scoundrel!" He got up and stood over Simon in a threatening attitude. Simon thought that Mr Ferguson was going to hit him. The veins on his forehead bulged and he was spluttering with fury.

"Father, are you going mad?" wailed Annabel.

Mr Ferguson, his eyes bulging, shook with fury, and took no heed of Annabel. "You will leave this house this instant. You will undertake never to see my daughter again. I absolutely and utterly refuse to allow you to see her. Marriage? Huh! My daughter is worthy of someone far above you."

White-faced, Simon stood up. He spoke quietly but firmly. "Mr Ferguson, I will go but with a heavy heart. Your daughter deserves a father who will try to make her happy. Today, you have destroyed her happiness."

"How dare you!" roared Mr Ferguson.

Simon ignored him and continued. "I ask for your daughter's hand in marriage not because I considered myself worthy of her but because I love her. I will go but I do not and will not promise never to see her. Let me remind you of what the scriptures say: 'Many waters cannot quench love, neither can the floods drown it'."

"If they could not make a text-quoting preacher of you they made a text-quoting teacher of you," sneered Mr Ferguson. "Well, I can quote too: 'Children, obey your parents'."

"There is an answer to that, Mr Ferguson: 'Fathers, provoke not your children to wrath'."

"You are provoking me to wrath," bellowed Mr Ferguson.

"Begone, and never set foot inside this door again or I shall have the law after you."

Simon strode to the door, then checked himself and turned to Annabel who was sitting in frozen immobility in an armchair. "Annabel," – it was the first time he had used her personal name out of deference for Mr Ferguson – "I want you to remember that text: 'Many waters cannot quench love, neither can the floods drown it'. Goodbye." She looked up and smiled a watery smile. He turned and went out, closing the door slowly behind him.

All passion spent, Mr Ferguson slumped into his chair. His trembling lower lip betrayed the turmoil within. The eruption might be over but the volcano was far from inactive. His silence was brooding and ominous. It was not the calm after the storm.

Annabel still hadn't moved. She looked pinched and drawn, as if the past ten minutes had aged her ten years. Her eyes were moist and her face ashen. She grappled with bitterness, bitterness against her father for his violent prejudice and against Simon for his rashness. But bitterness was against her creed and contrary to her nature. She was by nature optimistic and resilient. But where was there room for optimism in the present situation? Yesterday she had been apprehensively optimistic. The early flowering of her relationship with Simon had brought the fragile promise of Spring but one withering blast had swept away the blossom. The fury of the wind had stripped the leaves off the tree. But surely new growth would form, new buds develop and new shoots sprout. At the moment the hope seemed forlorn and merely desperate, but still it was hope.

DIFFICULT WORDS

Page 76	– explicit	*plain and clear*
Page 77	– vindictive	*pursuing revenge*
	– controversy	*dispute*
	– infernal	*devilish*
Page 79	– immobility	*lack of power to move*
	– deference	*respect*
	– ominous	*threatening*

Chapter 17

SEPARATION

For Simon, the weeks following his disastrous visit to the Auchengarve manse were torture. Anger had subsided to resentment and resentment had collapsed into misery and self-pity. He saw himself as stupid – stupid ever to have thought that marrying Annabel was possible, stupid to have allowed a relationship to have developed, stupid to have caused a scene with her father, stupid to have thought that her father's resentment at the Free Church had abated. Why did everything have to be so complicated? Others did not seem to have the same hurdles to cross and traumas to endure.

His attempts to contact Annabel were doomed to failure. His first letter had not been answered. Neither had his second letter. Instead, he had a brief letter from Annabel's father informing him that he had torn up the two letters to Annabel and threatening him with legal action if he ever attempted to contact his daughter again. The feeling of utter impotence completed his misery. Thwarted and frustrated, he fumed helplessly. He was like a ship struck by a storm in treacherous waters. He knew where the desired haven was, but the sails had been ripped apart and the rudder damaged. Now he was wallowing among waves which threatened to capsize the vessel and at other times he was drifting towards dangerous whirlpools.

In desperation, he thought of going to the Auchengarve manse, but though he toyed with the idea he knew it was folly even to think of it. Waiting near the manse to try to catch an opportunity to speak to Annabel as she went out was more likely to prove successful, but how could he know when she would come out? Perhaps her father would not allow her to go out unattended. Anyway, how could he skulk around hour after hour, day after day? If he were seen, as no doubt he would be, he would be disgraced. No, that was just clutching at straws. What about asking someone else to visit the manse on some pretext and slip a letter from him to Annabel? But whom could he get to go on such a mission? How would a go-between be able to pass a message on? No, that was an idea strictly for romantic novels.

Out of the blue, Simon received a letter from Annabel. It lay on his desk in school one morning when he came into his classroom. How it got there was a total mystery to Simon. Though he did not press the point, none of the pupils responded when he asked if any of them knew the letter had come to be on his desk. He knew it was from Annabel even though he was not familiar with her writing. He could not have explained it, but he knew. He could not open and read the letter until the morning lessons were over. Never had a school morning lasted for so long. Every minute seemed an hour. His mind could not settle on his work. It was an effort to listen to the children reading aloud and he kept making silly mistakes in his calculations which caused the children to titter. He was both thankful and apprehensive when it was time for the lunch break.

With fumbling fingers he opened the letter and anxiously scanned the contents.

Dear Simon,
I have not been able to write to you or send a letter to you till now. I have no way of knowing how you are and of how you view our future, but I am confident that you remain true and loving. Every day, I meditate on the text which you quoted as you left me. 'Many waters cannot quench love, neither can the floods drown it'. My love is unquenched.

Simon, you will need that text to strengthen you, because I have devastating news: my father is sending me to India. He has a brother who is in business in India. I have only met him once that I can remember. My father has written to him asking him to look after me, to show me around India and to introduce me to marriageble young men! He is at the moment arranging for my passage on a ship and for suitable escorts. My uncle is in business in Calcutta.

My first reaction was to refuse to go. I might have been able to persuade my father that he was exposing me to the risks of climate, wild animals, disease and the journey. But the more I thought about it, the more I felt that this was not the right thing to do. My father would fling in my face the accusation that I was a hypocrite, being very religious in some ways and yet disobeying a parent and so disobeying God. In the Auchengarve manse I am a virtual prisoner anyway. I see no way in which our situation here can be improved. My presence at home only increases my father's determination to prevent our seeing one another far less marrying one another. It is like a disease preying on his mind.

Though I have become reconciled to it, you may not find it so easy. If you feel that God is showing us that we are not meant for one another, I will respect your decision. I do not believe that obstacles, however insurmountable they may seem, necessarily show us that we are on the wrong path. The Children of Israel were stuck between the Red Sea and the Egyptian army, yet they were in God's path.

I am determined to look on the bright side. I will be able, with some ingenuity, to write you more freely in India. It may be that my father will see things differently when I have been abroad for a while. When I return I will be more independent and mature than I am at present and he will find it more difficult to be so authoritarian and high-handed.

I have arleady started looking at maps of India. I am trying to get as many books about the country as I can so that I can read them on the voyage. Hopefully, I will be able to study some of the Indian languages when I get there. I know it may be difficult for a woman, but I hope that I can do some spiritual good to the poor Hindus while I am there.

I hope that you do not think from what I have been saying that I view going to India and being separated from you by thousands of miles lightly. It makes my heart break. I was very bitter after that terrible confrontation between you and my father but I have learned that no good comes from bitterness. Peace and blessing come through submission. Submission is never easy. It is much easier to be bitter.

Wives are to be submissive to their husbands. I am not by nature a submissive person, so perhaps God is teaching me to be a submissive person in preparation for marriage.

Simon, I may not see you for years. Remember always that I will be faithful to you. If anything should happen to me, remember the good times. May God watch over us both and keep us.

Yours ever,
Annabel

Simon sat at his desk, stunned. India, India. He could not take it in. Again he read the letter. A heavy weight seemed to descend upon his spirit. "I may not see you for years". Simon seemed to have been stretched even further on the rack. Yet again he read the letter and this time some of the despair seemed to lift.

Annabel was resolute and hopeful. Why should he mourn? Hadn't he been tortured before by the lack of communication between them? Now Annabel had been in touch with him and had good hopes of being able to contact him regularly. Why hadn't he clung so firmly to the truth of the text he had given to her when she pondered its truth so often? He felt ashamed of himself. Annabel had obviously been through a lot. There was already a maturity in her, a wisdom, a seriousness which allied to her sense of humour and spirited personality made her even more attractive to him.

That afternoon, Simon announced that the class would shortly begin to study India. The haunted, preoccupied look had gone. In its place was a positive, determined look. That evening he went to see the Reverend Gillespie. He was looking for information about the Free Church missions in India.

DIFFICULT WORDS

Page 80	– subsided	*decreased*
	– abated	*slackened*
	– traumas	*severe emotional upsets*
	– impotence	*helplessness*
Page 81	– skulk	*lurk around*
Page 82	– virtual	*not absolutely, but as good as*
	– reconciled to	*accepting of*
	– authoritarian	*giving orders*
Page 84	– allied	*linked*

Chapter 18

SUMMONED TO THE MANSE

The purposeful, bustling mood did not last long. As he learned of the great pioneer Baptist missionary William Carey of Serampore, of the brilliant scholar and linguist Henry Martyn, of Dr Alexander Duff of Calcutta who established the Church of Scotland mission there and pioneered Christian outreach through education, of Duff's fellow Free Church missionary Dr John Wilson of Bombay (this brought back memories of hearing Dr Wilson preach in Edinburgh) and of others seeking to establish the gospel in that great land, a growing restlessness filled him.

He had heard the names of these men before but he had had little idea of the opposition they had encountered, the discouragements they had experienced and the labour they had expended. Perhaps he had not really been interested, had never deep within been gripped with the vision and passion which possessed these men. Why had they endured ridicule at home and resentment abroad? Was it not because of their love for Christ and their desire for his glory? Why had they left good prospects and civilised comforts for hot, dusty, noisy, foul-smelling cities plagued with verminous beggars? Was it not because they loved lost souls? A new awareness of the teeming millions of India and the gross darkness and idolatry disturbed him deeply. Yes, there was a great need in Scotland. The Free Church was facing an enormous challenge. But there had also been a tremendous response to the challenge. Hundreds of churches had been built. Manses had been provided. Schools had been established all over the country. Did they have these in Hyderabad and Lahore? Did they have them in Allahabad and Nagpur?

As he brooded over India's spiritual darkness, he also fretted over his lack of communication with Annabel. All he wanted was to let her know that he would be faithful. He wanted her to be reassured. He wanted her to sleep soundly at night confident that he was hers.

❊   ❊   ❊   ❊

Despite his preoccupations with these matters. Simon's life continued as it had done and his routine was undisturbed. It was a great shock to him then when he saw the Reverend Ferguson's housekeeper hurriedly approaching the school. A knock came to the door and his heart raced. Why was she sent to the school? Or did she come to tell him secretly about some scheme hatched by Mr Ferguson to make even more certain that he and Annabel remained apart?

"Come in!" called Simon.

The door opened cautiously and Annie Reid entered. Her usually cheery round face was etched with shadows of gloom. Her eyes were red as if she had been crying. Mud and wisps of withered grass clung to the bottom of her long black skirts and she was breathing heavily, as if she had been running.

"Can ah hae a word wi' ye, Mr Shaw?" panted Miss Reid.

"Certainly. Just one moment. Class, I want you to turn to page thirty-one. Read to the end of page thirty-four and then look over the questions on page thirty-five. I want no noise while I talk to this visitor. Do you understand?"

"Yes, sir," came the chorus from the class. Despite some curious glances at Miss Reid, the class got down to work.

Simon motioned to Miss Reid to go out and then he closed the classroom door gently.

"Well, how can I help you?" he asked.

"Oh, Mr Shaw, ah've been sent by the Reverend Ferguson. He says that he wants ye tae come tae the manse as soon as ye can. That's a' ah can say."

"But what is wrong? Has something happened? Is Miss Ferguson safe? Has anything happened to Mr Ferguson?

"Mr Shaw, ah canna tell ye ony mair. Mr Ferguson made me promise nae tae say onything tae ye.

"But I must know," insisted Simon. "I have a right to know. Why should I go to the manse when I don't even know why I have to go?"

Miss Reid had been too well trained as a servant to be persuaded. "Ah dinna ken aboot that, Mr Shaw, but ah ken fine that ah will lose ma job if ah tell ye. Ah hae been wi' Mr Ferguson a lang time. Ah had better nae keep ye frae yir class."

Miss Reid turned as if to go but Simon caught her by the arm. "Tell me, Miss Reid, is Annabel safe?"

She turned her gaze away from him. "Ah canna tell ye!" she burst out. "Jist go tae the manse tae find out." With that, she pulled her arm free and scuttled off. Simon was sure he heard a sob burst from her lips as she hurried across the play area.

It was with a heavy heart that Simon turned back to the classroom. All that day, a day to be engraved on his memory forever, time seemed like a boat rowing against the tide: it moved but seemed to make little progress. As if sensing his mood, the children were very subdued. Gloom seemed to pervade the school.

✳   ✳   ✳   ✳

He was reminded of the last time he had walked up the drive to the manse. Then, too, he had been filled with a sense of foreboding. Then, as now, the bare-branched trees chilled him and the manse seemed to loom ahead ominously.

He tried to calm himself and dismiss his fears. Mr Ferguson would not want him of all people if something had happened to Annabel. Mr Ferguson would probably lay all the blame on him in an orgy of loathing. No, it must be something else. Perhaps Mr Ferguson had been diagnosed as having an incurable illness which meant that he would die before Annabel returned from

India, never seeing her again. But why would he send for Simon in that case?

It was only as he rang the bell that Simon realised that all the blinds in the manse had been drawn.

"Come in, Mr Shaw. Mr Ferguson is waiting for ye." Miss Reid almost choked over the words.

She led him into the study. There a disturbing sight greeted Simon. Mr Ferguson sat hunched near the window with his back to Simon. The study which had been kept meticulously had an air of neglect. Books which were once Mr Ferguson's pride and joy lay gathering dust in heaps. On the great mahogany desk lay a small Bible, worn at the edges, and nothing else.

"Mr Ferguson, here is Mr Shaw tae see ye."

Mr Ferguson made no movement and said nothing.

Simon walked over to him. Mr Ferguson groaned and half turned round. He seemed to have shrunk. His face was grey and unshaven. He mumbled to himself.

Had Mr Ferguson gone mad? "Mr Ferguson, you sent for me. You wanted to see me", Simon said slowly, as if talking to someone who was too ill to comprehend.

"Yes," sighed Mr Ferguson. There was a silence.

"Mr Ferguson, is there anything wrong? Is your daughter safe?"

An awful groan seemed to come from deep within Mr Ferguson's breast. He gripped his head in his hands. "Annabel", he moaned. "Annabel lies at the bottom of the sea. Annabel is drowned."

Simon was stunned. All his forebodings had not prepared him for those devastating words. Before that point in time, his future had seemed to him like a rocky and uncharted landscape. Now that landscape appeared as if ravaged by a marauding army whose scorched earth policy had left it utterly ruined.

He fought against it but could not prevent the morbid thoughts which coursed through his mind. He could not exorcise the images which haunted his mind, images of Annabel drifting darkly through the depths of the sea, images of sodden

G

skirts and sea-greyed lace stirring in the cold currents, images of
prying sea creatures and, worst of all, images of Annabel with
staring, protruding, unseeing eyes and a face bloated and dis-
torted by salt water.

"Mr Shaw, ye had better sit down," said Miss Reid who had
stood waiting. Simon did not know how long he had stood there
lost in his thoughts, saying nothing. He pulled himself together.

"Mr Ferguson, I offer you my deepest sympathy. You must be
terribly distressed by this tragedy. I hope you do not blame me for
Annabel's death. I know that you do not approve of me, so it was
very good of you to tell me of your daughter's death personally.
However, my presence must be painful to you and I will not
prolong my stay. May God comfort you," said Simon, rather
stiffly and awkwardly.

"Stay!" cried Mr Ferguson. "I want to talk to you. Miss Reid,
you can go now."

The housekeeper made her way out unobtrusively and Simon
sat down.

"Do you see these books?" asked Mr Ferguson with a gesture
of his arm. Simon nodded. "What use are they to me? What
comfort can Aeschylus bring me? I have finished with them."

"Why did you bring me here?" asked Simon. "You could have
asked Miss Reid to tell me or you could have written a letter and
asked her to deliver it to me."

Mr Ferguson shook his head. "You were wrong when you
thought that I might blame you for Annabel's death. I did have
one wild spasm of hate for you, but that lasted only for a moment.
I sent her away, not you, and I have only myself to blame. I almost
changed my mind when I saw her go up the gangway to the ship.
She was always a bright and spirited girl, and when I saw how
fragile and forlorn she looked, a pang struck my heart. But my
pride would not let me relent." His shoulder heaved with silent
sobs. Simon pitied him. Was this the man who had erupted in
fury in this very room?

Simon's mind was in a whirl. What a cruel twist circumstances had taken! Mr Ferguson's love had destroyed the daughter he loved. What sort of a love was that? Was it as much jealousy and possessiveness which had fuelled Mr Ferguson's rage against him as scorn for his relatively humble background and resentment of his adherence to the Free Church? Was this an attempt by Mr Ferguson to discharge his guilt by confessing to Simon? Was he seeking Simon's forgiveness?

Simon hovered between anger at Mr Ferguson for the pride and obstinacy which cost Annabel her life and pity for a pathetic soul racked by grief and self-accusation.

"Mr Ferguson, like you I am overwhelmed with grief. I feel completely numbed. I cannot take it in. More than Annabel perished in the sea. My hopes for our future died with her. You find it difficult to forgive yourself, so you will appreciate that I find it difficult to have a forgiving spirit. All I know is that God can forgive. He dwells with him who has a humble and a contrite spirit."

Mr Ferguson looked searchingly into Simon's eyes. "Annabel said she loved you. She said that you were a good person and a true believer. Mr Shaw, pray for me. I am in despair. I need your prayers."

Simon felt moved. A lump formed in his throat. He nodded. "Mr Ferguson," he said, "I will pray for you but you need to pray for yourself. It cannot have been easy for you to have spoken to me like this. I appreciate it. I am only heart sorry that it has taken the death of the one we both loved to break down the barriers." Simon stood up. "I will go now. I want to be alone for a while. Has Annabel's body been found?"

"No," said Mr Ferguson. "The sea may never give up its dead but she died when the ship went down with all hands in a storm in the Bay of Biscay. Perhaps she will be washed ashore somewhere. I will tell you of any memorial service."

Though his eyes were wet and his face lined with grief, Mr Ferguson's grasp was firm and warm as he shook hands with Simon.

"Do not disturb Miss Reid. I will show myself out. God be with you."

Simon made his way out quietly. At the end of the driveway he went through the great pillars and, after leaning his head on one of them, wept bitter tears.

DIFFICULT WORDS

Page 85	– verminous	*full of vermin e.g. lice*
Page 86	– etched	*drawn in deep lines*
Page 87	– pervade	*spread through*
	– foreboding	*feeling that something bad is going to happen*
	– orgy	*unrestrained outburst*
Page 89	– meticulously	*with careful attention to detail*
	– ravaged	*laid waste or destroyed*
	– marauding	*raiding and plundering*
Page 90	– protruding	*sticking out*
	– bloated	*swollen*
	– unobtrusively	*so as not to be noticed*
	– Aeschylus	*an Ancient Greek dramatist*

Chapter 19

NEW DIRECTION

Simon came home from the memorial service comforted. Up till then it had been so hard. No-one knew the depth of his feeling because no-one knew the depth of his love for Annabel. Because he could not openly court Annabel he had been reticent about talking about her to anyone. Though he knew his parents were aware that he was attracted to her, he had said little to them. His Mum had been sceptical. "Aye, Simon, ye can forget her, like ah told ye a lang time ago. The Reverend Ferguson will have his eye on some laird's or colonel's son for her." The country people were sharp-eyed and could put two and two together but all they knew was that the young Free Kirk schoolmaster was keen on the Auld Kirk's minister's daughter.

What had comforted him was the words of Scripture read during the service: 'Many waters cannot quench love, neither can the floods drown it.' It must have been Mr Ferguson who had asked for it. Perhaps he remembered that they had been the last words which Simon had spoken to Annabel. Perhaps the words had a new significance for Mr Ferguson, just as they had for Simon. The many waters of the Atlantic could not quench his love for her, not could the floods of the Bay of Biscay drown it. Time might dull his grief but not his love. How precious that verse was to him. Hadn't Annabel quoted it to him in her last letter to him? How often had it brought comfort to her? Would he ever think of Annabel without thinking of that verse? Would he ever see the waves of the sea without thinking of it?

* * * *

Months passed and the restlessness of spirit which he had

experienced before the news of Annabel's drowning returned and deepened. The routine of teaching was carried out meticulously. To others it might have seemed that he was burying himself in his work to try to escape from his sorrow. But he found it unsatisfying, even irksome at times. It had become too routine. It no longer stimulated him. He had gone through a harrowing time of sorrow. He believed that he had come out from that experience stronger, unlike Mr Ferguson, who was a broken man. God had kept him. God had brought him sorrow but taught him faith. God had comforted him with the comfort of his Word. Was there not a purpose in that?

The truth was that his horizons had widened. The love for his own people and their ways remained with him, but he saw himself as having been as blinkered as any of the Clydesdales on his father's farm. Unblinkered now, he saw that there were other fields to plough and sow with the good seed of the gospel.

"Faither." he said one evening as he went out with his Dad to check the new-born lambs, "ye nivver intended me tae follow ye on the fairm, did ye?"

"Ye're richt there, Simon. It's a hard life an' a gey uncertain ane. It's aye diseases on this an' pests on that. Cattle get sick an' lambs get taken by foxes. Floods can droon the fields. Rain an' hail can turn a harvest field intae a soggy mess. Ah've seen a winter storm whip the roof aff a barn. Aye, it's no for the likes o' ye."

"Ah ken that fine, Faither, but whit is for me?"

Simon's Dad looked at him sideways. "Whit dae ye mean? Ye're happy teaching' in the schule, are ye no?"

"Ah mean that ah dinna think that teaching here is my real calling. Ah believe that God in his providence has planned it otherwise."

Simon's Dad stopped and looked thoughtful. "Ah see," he said, "Ah' whaur dae ye think God is callin' ye?"

"Tae India."

"Whit! Tae India?" His Dad was totally taken aback.

"Aye, tae India."

"Ah'm fair flabbergasted. Whit made ye think o' India?"

"When Annabel – Miss Ferguson – was sent tae India, that made me think aboot the country an' ah started tae find oot about it. Ever since then ah cannae get it oot o' ma mind."

"Perhaps it's jist a reaction. Ye maybe hae no got richt ower her drownin' yet."

"Faither, ah've thocht o' that. These are the daft ideas which are spawned by grief. Soon the notion grows cauld an' in no time is forgotten. But as each day passes, ah feel the urge tae bring the gospel tae the Hindus grow sharper and sharper within me. Ah cannae rest content teachin' here when millions hae niver heard o' Christ."

"It's a' very well tae pity the heathen, but there's a lot mair tae think o'. How wid ye survive the heat and dust? There will be nae doctors there an' a' sorts o' strange an' deadly illnesses. It wid be years afore ye learned the language. Ye'll be a stranger in a strange land. Ye could be like Miss Ferguson and die afore ye reached there."

"Faither, other missionaries hae gone wi' the gospel tae India. Ah'm sure that they heard a' these arguments as well. Dr Duff wis shipwrecked twice on his first voyage tae India and arrived wi' only his clothes and his Bible. That still didnae discourage him. Did Christ nae tell us, 'Go ye into all the world and preach the gospel to every creature'? Every time Mr Gillespie preaches, something speaks tae me. Last Sabbath morning ah wis given much encouragement when he preached on the text, 'On this rock will I build my church and the gates of hell shall not prevail against it.' Ah had been thinkin' tae masel that ah wid be nae use in India. Whit could ah dae against a' that superstition? But as he preached ah saw that it wis God's will that counted an' it wis God's power that wid convert the heathen in India, nae mine. A' ma objections hae been answered like that. When God calls, we may object like Moses did, but still we hae tae obey the voice o' the Almighty."

"Aye, ye're richt there, Simon. I canna argue wi' that."

"Besides, Faither, it'll be up tae the Kirk tae decide if ah hae the gifts an' if India's the place for me. But ah believe God wants me tae volunteer."

"Ye'll be a sair miss if ye go tae India, but ah widnae staun in yir way. If the Lord is calling ye, the Lord will keep ye. Yir mither will break her hert. Fur a' that she hadnae ony time fur books, she wis michty proud o' haein' a son a teacher."

"Ah ken that fine. Nae doubt there will be days ah will pine fur a glimpse o' yir faces if ah reach India. But we all hae tae part some time or ither. Ah ken the pain o' partin' mair than maist people."

"This past while has seen its fair share o' wrenches," said Simon's Dad. "There wis the partin' o' the ways wi' the Auld Kirk which wisnae done lichtly. There wis the tragic droonin' o' Miss Ferguson. Now there is the prospect o' partin' wi ye. Be that as it may, ye can be sure o' this: though ah widnae see yir face till eternity, ye will leave wi' ma blessin'."

The two men stood there as the sun set in the west and the light of evening grew dimmer. The bleating of sheep and the occasional cry of birds were all that was to be heard. There was a moment of profound peace between the two men. Their respect for one another ran deep. Eternity filled their thoughts.

"Christ said to another Simon, 'Feed my sheep'," said Simon's Dad, almost to himself.

"Aye," said Simon. "I believe that Christ has sheep in India. But where are the shepherds?"

"Come," said Simon's Dad. "Ah'm no real shepherd, just a bit fairmer wi' a few sheep, but at least ah'll teach ye that ye hae tae look after the lambs of the flock."

"Aye," said Simon, glad that he had spoken to someone at last about the burden on his spirit for India, "it'll be just the first o' mony lessons ah'll hae tae learn."

DIFFICULT WORDS

Page 93	– reticent	*holding back*
	– sceptical	*doubting*
Page 94	– irksome	*tiresome or wearying*
	– harrowing	*distressing*
Page 95	– flabbergasted	*completely astonished*

GLOSSARY OF SCOTS WORDS

a'	all	ken	know
aboot	about	kirk	church
afore	before	lang	long
agin	against	lichtly	lightly
ah	I	ma	my
ain	own	masel	myself
airm	arm	mair	more
alricht	alright	maister	master
amang	among	mither	mother
ane	one	mixter-moxter	topsy-turvy or disorganised
auld	old		
awa	away	mony	many
aye	yes or always	nae	not
bid	told or ordered	neeps	turnips
bide	put up with	nicht	night
canna	cannot	niver	never
dinna	do not	noo	now
dochter	daughter	o'	of
evra	every	oot	out
bletherin'	gossiping	ower	over or too
breeks	trousers	o't	of it
cairt	cart	richt	right
cam	came	saft	soft
cauld	cold	sair	sore
cope	overturn	shouldnae	should not
coup	overturn	sic	such
dae	do	tae	to
droon	drown	tak	take
evra	every	tatties	potatoes
fairm	farm	thocht	thought
fairmer	farmer	twa	two
faither	father	verra	very
frae	from	weel	well
galavant	wander about	wheesht	be quiet
galoot	stupid person	whit	what
gey	very	weans	children
gie	give	wi'	with
gowk	fool	wid	would
guid	good	widnae	would not
hae	have	wi' oot	without
hale	whole	wis	was
heid	head	wisnae	was not
hussies	impudent women	wrang	wrong
ither	other	ye	you
jist	just	yir	your

SOME OTHER KNOX PRESS TITLES

CHRISTIAN BASICS
Bible Studies on Christian Belief

This booklet has nine studies dealing with the Bible, God, Humanity, Jesus: Person, Jesus: Mission, Salvation, Holy Spirit, Church, Future. It is useful – (1) As an introduction to what Christians believe. (2) In a Bible Study Group designed to introduce people to the Christian faith. (3) In helping new Christians to grow in knowledge and understanding of the Scripture.

24 pages, booklet, 95p

NEAR INDIA'S HEART
Anne M. Urquhart

Near India's Heart is the record of the Free Church of Scotland's witness at the centre of India in the 20th century. The facts, carefully researched, are clearly presented. But this is more than an account. Having spent some 20 years in that country the author is able to convey a feel of life in India. Furthermore she does not fail to draw lessons from the development of the mission work that present a challenge to us.

Anne Urquhart, a medical doctor, was sent by the Free Church of Scotland to India in 1962. From 1975 she was seconded to the Emmanuel Hospital Association. She came home in 1984 and the following year was commissioned by the Foreign Board to research this account.

164 pages, paperback, £5.95

THE SHORTER CATECHISM
With Scripture Proofs and Comments by Roderick Lawson

'In the whole compass of Christian literature, apart from sacred Scripture, the Shorter Catechism holds a unique position... . There is no other document of its kind that presents the truth of the Christian faith with such precision of statement, such brevity of expression, such balanced proportion, such rythmical stylistic quality and such theological adequacy.'

'I know of no compendium of Christian truth that is more excellent than the Shorter Catechism, and what an inestimable reservoir of truth we possess if our memories are stored with and our minds established in the masterly definitions of that treasure of Christian literature.'

JOHN MURRAY
Professor of Systematic Theology,
Westminster Theological Seminary, 1937-66.

64 pages, booklet, 50p

For further information write to:
THE KNOX PRESS (EDINBURGH)
15 North Bank Street, Edinburgh EH1 2LS